The Mouhumes Jo

Copyright 2018 I C HEND

ISBN   SOFTCOVER   9781520106953

All rights reserved. No part of this story may be reproduced or transmitted in any form or by any means, electronic or mechanical, including photocopying, recording, or by any information storage and retrieval systems, without permission in writing from the copyright owner.

This is a work of fiction. Names, characters, places and incidents either are the product of the author's imagination or used fictitiously, and any resemblance to any persons, living or dead, events, or locales is entirely coincidental.

Acknowledgments

Elizabeth Reed

Sylvia Telford

Lillian Hall

Karen Henderson

Chapter 1

New Destinations

IT WAS A DARK STORMY NIGHT. The moon was hidden behind dark black clouds the rain was coming down hard. The weather had been horrible for three or so weeks: it had never stopped raining. The Mouhumes had been stuck in a small part of the park, in some woodland, for nearly two weeks. They had arrived there after being moved from the only home they had ever known. It had been in an area that had been untouched for years, plenty of fruits, berries and all sorts of other food.

The home the Mouhumes had once lived in had been turned upside down by big machines. Some Mouhumes had been sleeping, when their home was destroyed; many lost loved ones that night. It had been a large community, many generations and now, for all they knew they might be the only ones left moving from place to place, hoping to find somewhere they could settle down once again.

They had been on the move for what seemed forever, their leader Tube had taken ill so they rested and took advantage of the shelter in this small woodland. They had taken over a small rabbit warren on a sandy embankment. It was a good shelter from the wind and rain and because of the weather, food was in short supply.

The young Mouhumes wanted to go out on a hunting spree. They were dressed in fur from head to toe; Linden asked Ratty why they could not go out and gather food. Ratty could not explain why, however, he thought they should not go out hunting by themselves he just knew something was not right. Why had the rabbits moved away from the warren? All he knew was that there was a strange smell, a smell he had never come across before.

Ratty was exhausted. He had helped to dig part of the sandy embankment; they needed to make the room a safer place from the wind. The tunnel was larger than the Mouhumes would have liked but it had belonged to the rabbits, and rabbits are somewhat bigger than a Mouhume. Ratty just knew that it was not a night to be out in the dark, more importantly, they all needed some rest.

Unknown to them, this was going to be a night that would split them up forever. As they were resting some decided to go and look for food near the building in the car park. Some of the youngest had decided to go, they had often gone looking for food with Ratty, but this time Ratty was staying behind to rest.

Ratty who was named due to the way he caught and killed rats when he was younger, would nearly always go with the younger Mouhumes to help them learn how and where to find food but also to keep out the way of human's and their pets. He would sometimes take them into a human's house if they could not find food in other ways because he knew there was always food there. This also gave them the opportunity to watch the human's and discuss afterwards what they had learned.

The younger Mouhumes decided to sneak out and hunt for something to eat as they knew food supplies where running low. Ruddy and Mousey knew it would take more than just the two of them so they ran to see who else may be brave enough to go with them. Ruddy said Joy might go, but Mousey said the last time Joy went anywhere she ran off and Ratty had to end the hunting early. "What about Ellis?" No, said Mousey, he had a fright and was always reluctant to do anything that might be risky.

They took some time before they decided who they would ask and who they would not ask. Now they had to go and bring everyone together: They had picked ten in total: a good number so if they ran into trouble they had plenty of support to help each other. They separated to look around the burrow and to save time.

Mousey was heading towards where he thought Woozy might be. Woozy had a good sense of direction in the dark but was afraid of heights. On his way down the warren Jumper jumped onto his back and they rolled around the floor. Jumper was always doing this to keep his jumping ability up to scratch; well that's what he said. Mousey just thought he liked to show off. Mousey told him what they had planned and Jumper, without hesitation, agreed to go along with them.

Then Mousey told him that Ruddy was also coming, "a girl, what's a girl coming for?" Mousey told him that she had proved herself more than any of the others and she would be good if anything needed bashing. Jumper knew this and he also liked her a lot.

Ruddy and Jumper would often have fun together, they would roll around to see who was the strongest, Ruddy often won, but most of all without saying it, they liked each other so much; to see each other and to touch each other was good. He wished her no harm. Ruddy also liked

Jumper and that's why she had not mentioned his name when they were thinking about who to take with them.

They finally went around and spoke to everyone they thought would go with them. Some refused but others they had not thought of wanted to go with them. The ones who had not wanted to go said that it was too dark and wet and others said they preferred to go hunting and gathering food just as day was breaking. In the end only six in total would head out, not as many as they would have liked. "Six of them could do a fantastic job and bring a good meal" Scallop said who had also joined them.

Scallop was dressed in what used to be a uniform for a toy. It was from a toy soldier, a green camouflage outfit, the uniform was bigger than he was so he could put other undergarments on to help keep him warm, it made him look fatter than he really was.

Others had fur skins on from rats or other animals and like Scallop they would wear whatever they could find to help keep them warm and dry.

Ruddy was wearing a rat skin, she had helped Ratty kill it when they had gone out hunting. They did not like to leave anything they might be able to use, so the rat was skinned and the meat was eaten. Rats where a lot bigger than a Mouhume and they would kill a Mouhume if the Mouhume was alone, that's why they needed to go out in numbers to protect each other. With the fur pelt being bigger than Ruddy she found it easier to be able to move around and not be restrained in her actions, as some clothing slowed others down.

After a long discussion on where they were going to go hunting, they all agreed that the car park might be the best place as the large green area had not had any visitors there all the time they had been in the rabbit warren so there was less likely to be any food around left by humans.

Woozy wore some leaves stitched together. It had been his mothers' idea; she would also use sap from the trees, rubbing it over the leaves to help give it strength. It blended in well against the shrubbery and it was also waterproof. His mother often tried different ways of making clothes: in order to see which materials were the best suited for all weather types.

The car park was some distance away and it would take some time to get there. They would go along the riverside and keep in the hedge and under the foliage. The rain had flattened some of the plants, this would help to give them shelter from the rain and also anything that was on the prowl. Owls often came out around this time of night; they would swoop down taking mice and any other small animals. The Mouhumes had to keep their wits about them; other creatures hunting for food also came out in the safety of the dark, away from prying eyes.

Jumper wore baggy clothing made out of, what was once, a bath towel. It had been a dark red but now had lost most of its colour. Ruddy had changed; she was dressed, as ever, in a fur skin. This one was taken from a young rabbit, she said it was warm and waterproof to a point. Jumper liked his outfit; he said it would let him move without any restriction.

As they went along the riverside they played around. Like all young creatures, they liked to have some fun. Ruddy, the youngest, was also the fastest: she could climb a tree as fast as any cat. At the back of the group, she slinked away ever so quietly; she ran upfront waiting for the rest to come her way. She waited half way up a small bush, hidden away behind the leaves and slightly wet from the rain; she went as still as a statue. When the rest came beside her she leapt out off the bush and onto Jumper's back. He was the second oldest in the group, and as true to his name, he jumped high with Ruddy on his back; she clung on, laughing as she did so.

Mousey ran and hid under an old log, Scallop ran the other way and hid under some shrubbery, the other two: linden and woozy ran into each other and knocked each other down, knocking the wind out of each other. This was not the Mouhume way: they had been told when they have to hide; they should always keep away from one another but always know where each of the others were.

Ruddy, was still holding onto Jumper's back as he hopped and rolled around trying to get her off, he was still unsure what or who, was on his back. The others watched but still hid away, just to make sure they had not got any unwanted attention. Linden and Woozy eventually got to their feet and scurried under some shrubs together. Woozy always said that sometimes it might be better than being separated from each other.

Jumper finally got Ruddy of his back and ran up a small young tree to see what and who had attacked him. Hidden away he looked around and could see that Ruddy was lying on the ground laughing. He knew then that she had played one of her tricks on him and he would get her back later with a trick of his own.

She might be the only female in that food finding group but she was certainly one of the bravest. Ruddy would take on anything that she thought would harm her friends. He remembered the time they had been taken out on a hunting expedition with Ratty; they had came across a large and aggressive rat. It had Ratty in a corner and he had no escape, so Ruddy, without any thought for herself, ran up the side of a wall around the rat, almost pushing the rat with her hand before she landed on her feet then she stood in front of Ratty to protected him and screamed with such anger in her voice that the rat ran away quickly.

Jumper had seen this so many times from her that he could not count how many times she had saved one or more of the Mouhumes. Her bravery had often been talked about; however, she had one weakness, she often did things without thinking, things that could also put the others in danger.

Just then the others came out of their hiding places. Jumper knew he would have to say something, "Ruddy, if you don't stop fooling around you will be stopped from coming on these expeditions. Do I make myself clear?" Ruddy sunk her head into her chest and nodded slightly. She knew that danger was all around them but also she knew they had to have fun sometimes and finding the time for fun was hard.

As they approached the car park they looked around to make sure there was no risk to themselves. Near the car park there was a bungalow with a large garage joined onto it. They separated and scurried around, looking around but still in contact with each other. They went in pairs, one pair checked out an area and then the next pair moved forward so that they kept together. If they got into any trouble the others would be able to help or they could make a quick getaway.

They could often find some food that the humans had thrown away if they looked in the bins around the car park, This time, however, all the bins had been emptied so Mousey decided to go into the building. They found a small hole in the brickwork and soon they were all in the building. But unknown to them a cat lay asleep in the next room. The door was also slightly open so the cat could go out when it liked. They looked around the room, it had a large object with wheels they knew from past experience. Sometimes food had been dropped near these things when humans got into and out of them.

They continued to look around. There was a cage at the end of this room in the corner; it had an old carpet draped over it. Then Linden stuck his nose in the air, he had not smelled anything like this before so he beckoned to the others. They all came together and he said, ever so quietly, that he was afraid this smell was something to be wary off.

Ruddy asked if they should have a look to see what it was. But Linden said not to look; he was beginning to tremble with fear. Mousey held his arm out and took hold of Linden, pulling him away from the rest of them he asked him ever so calmly what was wrong. Linden could not say for certain but he knew whatever lay behind that carpet would be far worse than anything they had ever come across before. They could hear something thrashing around in a cage. It was trying to get out. It sounded like it was becoming more and more annoyed. It also sounded like it was starting to scratch at the cage door, as if it was trying to dig itself out.

Just then they heard a squeak from the door that was slightly open, they all hid in different places. The door opened, light from the doorway now shone into the garage. There were still dark areas but the Mouhumes could now see what was around them. Nothing came out from the door "the door must have just swung open by itself" said Jumper. As they moved around the garage they looked around to see if there was anything they could use or even eat. The noise from the cage was getting louder and louder, so they decided to be brave and go and see what was behind the carpet.

Jumper leaped onto the top of the cage, Scallop and Ruddy helped each other up then Woozy and Ruddy helped Mousey up. When they where all on top of the cage they pulled the carpet up; it was a hard task especially as they were just young Mouhumes.

The thing inside the cage was now more excited; it was pacing around the cage. They now had the carpet pulled all the way on top of the cage. Claws were now coming out from the wire mesh door. The smell was nothing they had ever smelled before. So they were unsure what to expect. It started to head butt the door and scratch under the gap at the door, it was determined to get out.

Woozy was standing on the edge of the cage when all of a sudden something grabbed hold of him and pulled him onto the floor; the rest of them looked over the side towards Woozy. Woozy lay lifeless on the floor.

The cat picked him up and started to walk away when Ruddy jumped from the cage onto it's back and pulled hard on it's whiskers as if she was riding a bull, just like a cowboy. The cat held on to Woozy with it's jaws. Ruddy then punched the cat in the side of it's eye, the cat give a loud growl and dropped Woozy onto the floor. Ruddy held on for her life as the cat ran, jumped and rolled over trying to get her off.

Scallop and Jumper went to Woozy and pulled him away to safety, Mousey and Linden without thinking pulled the catch on the cage door and opened it, thinking that the thing inside would attack the cat. The polecat jumped out of the cage and ran towards the cat. Linden called out to Ruddy. Ruddy turned her head to see the polecat running towards them. She jumped off and ran towards the hole in the wall.

Linden and Jumper ran to help Scallop and Mousey with Woozy. The polecat leaped onto Jumper and bit into his neck. The others knew he was gone, they scampered away knowing that they would have to recover his body.

Outside Ruddy was gasping trying to get her breath back when the others came out holding onto Woozy, she asked where Jumper was, they shook there heads. Ruddy with an all mighty scream ran back inside and with a sharp pointed stick she ran it into the side of the polecat. It dropped Jumper and ran a short distance away. Ruddy picked up Jumper's body, carried him over her shoulder and out the hole they had came in.

The others had gone back onto the riverside and hid under the shrubbery for cover. Woozy had starting to come around now. When the cat got hold of him he had passed out and this may have saved him. The cat probably thought he was dead so the cat would not go any further than hold onto its prey.

Ruddy was heading towards them carrying Jumper, all of a sudden Mousy saw the polecat coming out of the hole and heading towards Ruddy. Mousy also had a sharp pointed stick and ran towards the polecat. The polecat saw this and pounced towards Mousy; Mousy quickly moved to the left side and ran up and hid in a nearby bush. Mousy needed time to help Ruddy as she was exhausted. The polecat ran in to the bush looking for Mousy giving them valuable time to escape.

The rest quickly moved under the undergrowth for protection; the rain came down even harder as they moved along heading back to the camp. They came along a clearing when suddenly an owl swooped down and took hold of Jumper and flew away. It was often the case when a Mouhume had died, another animal would often devour the body. This was the Mouhumes way; this was how they never got discovered.

They started to head back to the warren knowing that Jumper's family would be devastated with the news that he had been taken from them. All of them were exhausted from the struggle they had just encountered. They now had to move quietly with speed but still be aware the polecat was on the prowl. They had to be cautious, not only the polecat but other hunters too would be out and about; the smell of a kill would attract all types of killers.

They heard a sound from the side of them, but luckily it was still some distance away. They stopped and listened to see what direction it was coming from. They still held the sharp sticks they first took out with them, these were ready to use, if needed. Whatever it was had also stopped. After standing for some time they moved slowly and quietly. Ruddy, the first to do so, she was upset and thought whatever it was, if it came to attack her she was ready and willing for a fight. Her eyes were full of tears, she found it hard to concentrate on what she was meant to be doing and all she could think was how Jumper had been taken away from her.

The sound came closer then suddenly a nose poked out of the foliage. Still with tears in her eyes and without any focus, she jumped onto the head of the polecat and started to scream and pierce its neck, it rolled around trying to get her off but she hung on then stuck the stick into its eye. The stick broke and she fell off, it ran away bumping into everything in its way. The others came but Ruddy continued to run after the polecat with what was left of the broken stick in her hand.

Linden called for her … but nothing came back; Linden tried to smell the air to see what was round them. The damp air was full of strange aromas that he had never smelled before; he just knew that danger was all around. Just then a noise came from the direction that Ruddy and the polecat had gone, a scuffle and screams and then a deadly silence. Mousey's heart sank.

The others came back to join him but he insisted they should carry on back to camp to warn the others. Then the sound of the crackling from broken sticks and things on the wet ground could be heard and suddenly out from the shrubbery came Ruddy, with blood dripping from her. Her fur clothes ripped and chunks of fur missing, she fell to the ground, Scallop and Woozy ran to her aid.

They picked her up and ran they hid under a large prickly bush for protection. By now they were all worn out physically and mentally through fear, they could not see how they could get back and if they did, they might take danger back to the camp.

What could they do? Mousey said they needed to catch their second breath and get anything they could use to protect themselves. Scallop's head stretched up, he could hear something, so he signalled for them all to lie down, which they did. Under the fallen leaves and in the wet earth, they lay still, whatever it was looked into a bush not that far away from them. Luckily, the wind was blowing towards them and away from whatever it was. For now the danger had passed.

They still had a long way to go to get back to the camp. They could still encounter all sorts of danger but they knew if they did not at least try they would also lose Ruddy. Her body was now limp; she was not in a good way. Once full of fight, Ruddy was now lifeless. They started out with six, now there was only five and they all thought they might end up losing her. Jumper, who had been the leader that night, was now dead. Ruddy, who was their strength, was now all but dead herself. Could they make it back?

As they lay under a well established blackberry bush, with thorns and prickles, they had plenty to help protect them from any attack that might come from the sky and also from the ground.

Mousey was upset; after all he did persuade them to go into the building and now they were all at risk. Not that they had never been in this situation before but because now they did not have anyone who could help. None of them had the experience to take command; it was as if they had lost all hope when Scallop spoke up, "look we cannot stay here all night we must move and move soon".

"What about Ruddy? What can we do with her, she's heavy and when we are in the open we are in more danger," voiced Linden. Woozy's head was buried in Scallop's chest, he was crying. The thought of leaving Ruddy; after all, it was Ruddy who helped save his life. "No, no", then "NO" with an almighty scream "you cannot, no she saved me, please don't, don't".

"Quiet, quiet do you want us all to be killed?" Mousey said in a calm but persuasive voice. He knew that if they carried her they would be putting themselves at risk. Two of them would have to carry her and then take turns; none were strong enough to bear her weight, not like her. She would have picked anyone of them up and carried them and still have the strength to protect them. They knew they had to decide what to do with her: not an easy decision and one that could put them all in more danger. Any hunting trip always had that danger and there would be times there would be those who would not make it back.

Mousey then came up with the proposal: "We have two things that we can do, one leave her and hope that she, that she …" he stopped, the words would not come out, "… and the other is taking turns and carry her".

"We could stay here and one of us could go back to camp and get help," Scallop said with confidence in his voice.

"What happens if the one that goes for help gets hurt or worse, then what?" Linden asked. Feeling very worried that no one would make it back to camp at all. They all knew at this time of night every predator would be out hunting.

After what seemed a long discussion they decided that Woozy, Scallop and Mousey would go back to camp and leave Linden with Ruddy. This was the best thing to do. Woozy would be too afraid to stay by himself and Mousey could defend himself better than Linden could.

The rain had now stopped, the clouds had parted and the moon was almost full. This gave a good light to see and be seen. They would keep in the cover of the foliage that had been crushed by the rain. What once stood tall was now half the size but this would give them better protection. The density from some plants would make it harder for predators to spot them.

Linden being left alone was fearful, not just for himself but also for the other three who had a great distance to travel before they would be back at the new camp. He went to check on Ruddy. They had covered her with leaves to try and keep her dry and warm, she was so cold. Linden had no idea what to do; he had not been on many hunting expeditions. He tried to think about what they had experienced.

Now the rain had stopped all he could hear was the odd raindrop falling from the trees and branches. Suddenly there was a noise, a distinctive sound; something else was hunting, walking slowly and gently over the ground. What could it be? Linden stood up and moved closer to the external covering from the thorns that helped keep him secure from anything bigger than a Mouhume. Looking out from a clearing, he could see across the river. The hillside met the skyline. His eyes had to adjust to the difference in light and the sound of the night.

There were different animals in the distance: cows mooing in a field and sheep making the odd noise. It all sounded normal he thought but then suddenly a muzzle with big teeth was at his chest. He froze with fear. The teeth were now very close to his head, only the thorny bush stopping it getting any closer. This is it he thought, then suddenly a yelp from the animal, Ruddy stabbed the thing in its nose with a long thorn.

She then ran after it with a number of thorns. She was on a death mission, the animal yelped again, she must have stabbed it again and again, it made off yelping as it ran away.

Linden stood in the same position with fear; Ruddy came back and tapped him on the shoulder. "Hurry up", she said "we best be off before he comes back and eats us", she laughed. Linden could hardly believe his eyes, she was all but dead moments before and now she was back as if nothing had been wrong! She went out of sight for a moment and then back again in a flash. Her fur was ripped from earlier and it had bits missing. She looked tattered and yet she was full of spirit, what had got into her?

Linden was unsure but he knew if he had any opportunity to get back to the rabbit warren it was with her. She always had strength but now she had something else. This night she had taken on animals, who in their own right were killers, this was not something you would want to encounter even with numbers on your side but she took them on by herself and won.

A hand grabbed hold of Linden's arm, "hurry up" she whispered then she was off. Linden did not waste anytime; he hurried trying to keep up with her. Side by side they were moving in the undergrowth. Where did she get this energy from? Linden could barely keep up with her. She had to slow down so the distance would not grow too great from her.

A sound from up ahead alerted Ruddy, she stopped suddenly as she had been running. Linden who also had been running fast trying to keep up with her when she stopped promptly he carried on running into her, knocking her over.

She jumped to her feet then up the bush from one stem to the next. Linden had no idea what was happening. Why had she stopped? Why?

What had she seen? She was back down on the ground as quick as she had scaled the bush. Then she ran into the open space and onto the grass verge. She picked up a half eaten apple that a human had dropped; it was as big as she was. Linden ran over to help her. They started to eat into it.

After a short time they carried it between them heading back to the camp, moving quietly but with urgency, they headed back the same way that they had come.

Now that it was only two of them, Linden wondered if the others got back safely. Only time would tell. All Linden knew was that whatever they would encounter Ruddy would give them the edge. Linden realised why Ratty would always let her go on hunting expeditions, she was better than the male Mouhumes. He also knew that he would have to keep an eye on her; it was as if she was on a death mission.

Linden had heard Ratty talking about Ruddy once and now he knew what he had overheard was true, why she needed one of them to try and calm her down.

Ruddy was always being talked about by the other Mouhumes. She was almost a living legend. Mouhumes often would speak about how Ruddy had taken on creatures twice the size as her and always won. Now Linden had seen this for himself.

Suddenly Ruddy dropped the apple and was off. A thud and a squeal, Linden's thoughts were interrupted. Ruddy was on top of some creature. Linden ran to help, when he got to Ruddy, he realised she was on top of Ratty.

Ratty had came looking for them with a number of other Mouhumes, when they had came across Mousy and the others. They had told him what had happened. Ratty would have normally left an injured Mouhume to other creatures but he could not with Ruddy. She had saved many other Mouhumes without a second thought. He knew he would have lost his own skin a number of times had it not been for Ruddy and not just the one time the Mouhumes had talked about.

Ruddy jumped to her feet laughing, Ratty was covered in the wet earth. He cursed her and those around as they were all laughing. Some were holding onto their stomachs and some were rolling on the damp ground. It had looked ever so funny for them. Ruddy often made them laugh with her antics. Ratty wiped some of the mud from his side and plonked it on Ruddy's head. With mud rolling down her face, this made them laugh even more. Being little creatures, they could laugh quite loud.

It was time for them to head back to the rabbit burrow. Some of them were tucking into the apple. Before long it was all gone. The Mouhumes had seen some food on the way to find Ruddy so they would pick that up on the way back. As they approached the food they could sense that something was not right. They spread around, all in sight of each other. What could it be? A strange smell, a smell that they had never came across before. They were anxious more so than any other time. Even Ruddy was fearful, Ratty at this time, decided they should leave the food and beckoned to the others.

They all moved away silently, but one whose greed and curiosity had the better of him returned and went towards the food, not making any noise he grabbed a handful of food and ate it, he was just about to take hold of another handful when he fell to the ground dead. The food had been poisoned. A human must have placed the food there to kill creatures in that area. They had not known that it had been poisoned but Ratty's instinct had put them off trying the food.

The young Mouhume was now dead; his little body was left on the ground un noticed by the others. The poison might already have been amongst the junk that had already been there or even the park assistant might have put it there, as some of the waste had been attracting rats. The fact is the Mouhumes had not come across this before. Now this would be an added danger. Not just the day-to-day wildlife that often got in the way but also this group of humans. They would have new experience in a world that they never knew existed.

They still had some distance to go before they would reach the warren and nothing to take back. It had been a disappointing hunting expedition and a poor hunting party: nothing but tragedy and failure from start to finish. A lesson had been learned about this part of world they had come across. They would have to learn and learn fast if they were to survive. Those who were lucky enough to escape and find others had more chance of survival than those who were now by themselves. This small group was getting smaller day-by-day with the new surroundings and new dangers they had never encountered before.

They had tools and weapons. They used thorns from the thorn bushes: they would snap them off the bush whilst they were still growing at the beginning of the year then dry them off in the hot sun to harden them. There was also a gooseberry bush with thorns that were long and sharp. It did not just supply them with food but also the tools and weapons that they needed to survive. Mouhumes learnt from an early age.

Everything they had known had been destroyed; they would now have to pool all their resources and skills together if they were to continue to exist.

Chapter 2
Back at the warren

Tube came to see them, he was not happy that they had gone without permission. This small group that went out hunting had lost lives, not just from those who had gone but also from those who had went looking for them.

Tube asked to see Ruddy, she was now in the lower part of the warren. She had gone to a little hole that she had scraped out from the soft sand, a small hole just big enough for her to squeeze into

Ruddy's energy was low due to the fighting that night and lack of food. She had no idea if, when she fell asleep would she wake up, part of her hoped that she would not. She had lost the love of her life. Just as she was going into a sleep she heard a voice. "Ruddy…Ruddy…are you awake…wakeup Ruddy you're needed…hurry" With her eyes squinting she looked towards the voice, once again the voice asked if she was awake

Ruddy jumped to her feet and got hold of the arms of the young Mouhume and pinned him to the ground. "Please let go…Tube asked me to come and see if you were ok and if you would come to the meeting area." The young Mouhume had heard stories about Ruddy but when seeing her lying all helpless and almost dead like he thought that's all they must have been…stories. But when she jumped up and held his arms and had him on the ground before he knew what was going on, he then knew that the tales were true

Unknown to Ruddy she had been asleep for almost a day and a half, Tube needed to see her. She had been the topic of conversation and not all good. Some of those who had been talking about her, were afraid of her and wanted her out the colony by any means. Even if it meant to kill her but Tube knew that they needed her more than she needed them.

He was defending her against some more of the younger and stronger Mouhumes. Ratty was telling them she had saved more lives than any other, if she was to go he would go too. She had also saved his life and there would be a great number of Mouhumes who would probably go as well

The Mouhumes who had wanted her to go said that she would have to go quietly, as they could not lose any more Mouhumes from the colony. They new the colony would become weak if any other Mouhumes left with Ruddy

Ruddy entered the large room with the young Mouhume at her side. The young Mouhume was asked if she had come willingly. "Yes" the young Mouhume replied "Ruddy put up no resistance"

Ruddy started to wonder what was going on. The young Mouhume stood back, just at the side of Ruddy. His hand went into his fur cover. Ruddy could see that his hand was on a sharp thorn similar to what she had often used herself. She could see the council talking quietly. The only two she knew there was Tube and Ratty. The others had taken charge when they had found the rabbit warren, purely through numbers and aggression.

Tube was the leader but these young Mouhumes were now taking over. It was clear to see, Rug dressed in bits of old bits of fabric came forward. He was a big strong Mouhume he had a number of other Mouhumes at his side. He spoke out loud.

"Ruddy we have all decided that you should go. You are not welcome here anymore you have made to much trouble; we have lost too many Mouhumes with your actions. Collect your things and go without telling any of the others"

Ruddy looked around the room there must have been thirty Mouhumes if not more, all against her, she knew some would do this but others she never thought they would do any harm towards the colony, even Tube and Ratty stood without saying anything. They must be standing down from the position they had held as leaders. She had never known this to happen in the history of Mouhumes

"Do you not hear me go now or you will be put to death" Rug's voice filled with anger it was as if he wanted Ruddy to rise to the bait. He could see that she was worn out, she was as thin as a twig and she had little if any strength left. Ruddy started to walk away, back towards her area where she had left all her things. She could hear them laugh at her and then came a voice.

"You go now we need what ever you have, you go as you are" then more laughter

Ruddy stopped in her tracks. Just for a moment the young Mouhume, who had woken her, stood with a worried look on his face, Ruddy smiled at him then walked on heading towards the way out. The young Mouhume walked towards her his hand moved inside his over coat, towards the weapon Ruddy had seen him place there

As Ruddy got out of sight from the others the young Mouhume pulled the weapon out Ruddy jumped back giving herself some distance, there was a look of surprise on both their faces. He was handing it to her with the handle towards her. He told Ruddy he had been told what might happen and that he should give her something to help her, he then handed her some food.

"There had been talk for some time that the Mouhumes who had told you to leave were trying to take over. They knew that Tube wanted to move out of the warren. They thought that they should stay and they also knew you would protect Tube and Ratty. They decided to tell you now because you are at your weakest"

Ruddy took the weapon from the young Mouhume and the food. Then off she knew that she would not be safe. As she went around the next bend in the warren she was met by a number of Mouhumes, all with there own belongings

Must have been twenty or more, Tube and Ratty were also there, they said that they would have to hurry as if those left in the warren knew what they were doing they would try and stop them leaving.

Ratty and some of the others took food supplies and some of the weapons that they would need. They had not taken a lot of food; just enough that they could carry. Each one had a little pouch not much bigger than a fist attached to a piece of string holding together what ever over coat that each Mouhume was wearing. Ruddy was then told that the other Mouhumes had sneaked out from some of the holes away from the others, after all it was a big warren.

The larder in the warren was away from the area that held the meeting. They had left enough food for those who were too afraid to leave with them, but those who had left knew it was the right thing to do.

Chapter 3
Departure

NOW THEY HAD to decide which way to go: over the river or up the steep hill? On the other side of the river they could see woodland and up the hill houses. The river was running fast from the rain so that would be out the question.

Up the hill there would also be danger but between the two, the hill would really be the only way to go. They could not go back to the warren as the Mouhumes now in charge would most likely kill Ruddy and one or two of the others.

It was still light so they would have to keep under cover. There were trees and a hedge running along up towards the top of the hill and there were areas where they had some ground cover, but parts with no cover at all.

They decided the hedge would be the better way to go. At least they could stay out of sight from humans and any prying eyes, such as wild birds of prey.

It was a long way to the top of the hill. Once they got to the top there was a road: cars were running in both directions. The Mouhumes had only seen cars a few times before in the car park but they had always been parked or moving slow. These cars where moving fast, how could they get to the other side?

Just then they heard a noise. Humans, they were jumping around with each other. There was also a strange smell. What could it be? The humans were carrying paper, putting their hands in, then pulling something out and eating whatever was in the paper.

The Mouhumes watched in amazement. It must be food! As the humans got near, things were dropping out of their hands and onto the ground. The smell was the same as what was in the air. All of a sudden one of them ran towards one of the others and threw his package towards the other humans head, laughing as he did so; the contents fell to the ground. The humans all ran off. This was not that much different to how the Mouhumes sometimes carried on, apart from, they would never waste food.

Some of the Mouhumes had been so hungry that as soon as the humans were out of sight they ran towards the food. They picked it up, dropping it just as quick as it was hot. What was this food?

Suddenly a crow swooped down. Then others came. The Mouhumes quickly ran under a prickly bush. The crows, now around eight or ten, were eating the chips on the ground. Some were ripping the chip paper open to get the chips that were still wrapped up. The Mouhumes remained hidden.

Darkness was creeping in. The car lights were now turned on. This was strange for the Mouhumes. The crows were eaten the last few scraps. The Mouhumes had a sinking feeling there would be no food left the crows had eating all the chips.

The Mouhumes who were still on the other side of the road could not cross over. The road seemed to be getting more and more cars coming from both directions. They had to stay separated for longer than they wanted. The coming and going of the cars slowed down, then for a short time stopped. The rest of the Mouhumes finally crossed the road. They ran as fast as they could straight into the shrubbery. There were a number of houses on that side of the road with fences around the gardens. Some had sheds. The Mouhumes knew they had to find shelter before it was completely dark.

The nearest houses were over a grass hill which was in the open. They would have to go now if they were going to go there. There were semi-detached houses with trees around the back and small front gardens.

The shrubbery was not large enough to hide them all so they would have to be quick to decide what to do. They made a dash in small numbers to the first house. It had a fence around it but had gaps big enough for any small animal to go through; even a full grown rabbit would not find it difficult to go through the fence.

In the yard at the back of the house there was a coal bunker. The Mouhumes had never seen a coal bunker. The hatch was open and lucky for them not a lot of coal inside. Darkness was setting in. The bungalow had its lights on, giving a glow outside. Not that the Mouhumes needed any lighting to see, they had good eyes, even in the dark.

The coal bunker was not big enough for all the Mouhumes to be safe and sound and out of sight. Some of them ran to the tree that had some of its roots raised above the ground. They hid under the roots. There was more than enough room as there had been some earth dug away. Others hid under a shed in another garden. At this stage they had no idea of gardens, homes or anything else that belonged to those who lived in the houses but they would soon find out the benefits of hedges and fences that ran around the different properties.

They needed to rest. They all carried little bits of food they had been given or had taken from the rabbit warren. Some would have to share as others had not had time, or the opportunity to collect anything.

Some came for the adventure; others knew they could not stay at the warren because they knew the Mouhumes had been split. They also knew the leadership was being questioned by a reckless young Mouhume who would never want anyone in his group that might have an opinion or those that might have high regards for Tube, Ruddy and any of the others that were highly respected or had any status. Now they were just trying to survive and find somewhere that they could settle down, not just for the night but for the future.

After a while Tube called for the senior Mouhumes, those who held some sort of rank. He was aware that some had stayed at the warren. There were still a strong few who had proven themselves again and again, one more than most, Ruddy. She was something special. She hardly ever questioned his commands. She had the intelligence only to question when she thought she needed to and she could fight with speed and agility to get out of almost any danger.

Ratty was one of the first to come along with a number of others. Tube looked around, one was missing. He took a deep breath that was almost a sigh. What was she up to now? It was not the time to worry he had to tell the others his thoughts. Tube knew it was not safe, a rest would be ok but he himself had never been in such close contact with humans before or the buildings that they lived in. Tube explained that he thought it was best to move on. They had rested for a while, longer than he intended. Now it was time to decide which way they would go.

It was dark. Some of the lights that had been lighting the homes had now gone out. One or two in the distance still had a glow from up above on big poles. The Mouhumes had never seen such things. It was a lot to take in. These were new dangers.

After a short discussion they decided to go up towards the hill. Unknown to them, they were going deeper into a housing estate but from where they were they had little choice. Rug and the other Mouhumes were down that hill, along with other dangers.

It had been an unwritten rule: that Mouhumes did not kill another Mouhume unless other Mouhumes lives were in danger. Yet Rug seemed like he would kill anyone who got in his way. So Tube did not want to go back, he did not want Mouhumes fighting with each other.

They collected what things they had and what might be useful later. Then suddenly Ruddy was back with a bag full of food. She had been on a bird table and taken little bits of allsorts that were there. She had picked up a small bit of cloth rolled it out and filled it with as much as she could carry.

It was shared around. Ratty gave her a smile but he knew Tube would be slightly angered as he did not want any of them wandering around this new world without help, or another Mouhume to at least warn the others.

They decided now might be the best time to move on again. The streets were almost empty apart from the odd car. Some of the Mouhumes had been covered in coal dust from the bunker. They were as black as night. Ratty saw this as good camouflage. They could go in and out of the hedges and not be seen by any humans or any other potential danger; but not all the Mouhumes wanted to be covered in this dust so they stayed as they were with whatever they had.

They moved in groups of six or eight depending on age and ability. They all went the same way leaving a little distance between them. Some were as fast as lightning and others hesitated so were just a little slower, some were just reckless, like Ruddy, but it all worked because no doubt, as things happen no matter how fast or even hesitating only experience might get them out of a life or death situation.

They started to move further up the hill not knowing where it would take them. Ruddy was in front followed by Ratty who was finding it hard to keep up with her. He wondered what was driving her. It had not been that long she was at death's door and now, as always, she was determined.

Tube had put together the teams, knowledge, strength, then speed – the first troop had been mostly strength to overcome any danger and deal with it and fast enough to go back to help any other group that may need a helping hand. The middle group was mixed with young and old, experience and youth. The two groups either side were strength and again age but would be able to help the old and young Mouhumes, if needed.

Those who had been in the coal bunker were as black as coal. The damp dust clung to the clothing that they had on which in turn made them harder to see. They were like shadows, creeping in and out of the shrubs. They had never seen coal but soon found out the benefits of the dust.

They had to go across another road. This would be the second road they had ever crossed. Unlike before, it was now quiet. There was no traffic but they still went with uncertainty.

The sky was dark. The half moon was behind clouds. Street lights were giving off light. This was not something the Mouhumes wanted so they went quickly into gardens where they could hide in flower beds and other shrubbery.

They had no idea what they were looking for but they would know when they got there or found it. Ideally no houses, just woodland would be the best place for them: a place that would cover and feed them and protected them from danger.

They had travelled through many gardens and were getting tired. They needed to find cover. Morning was coming it was starting to get light and they would have to go out of sight.

In the distance they could hear running water. This was never a bad thing as they would need a drink. They would often just go under a plant, depending on the type. It might be a flower that might hold water. Therefore, they would tip it and let the water pour into their mouths. Sometimes they even got washed this way whether it was intentional or not.

Ruddy was with Ratty. Ratty was not going to let her run off into what might be danger. He was not holding her back by her arms, but it was emotionally exhausting having to watch her. It was like trying to hold a wild bull back. She was ready to run off into the distance, wanting to see what was there. She always wanted to see what was around the next corner or what was over the hill.

Just as he thought he had her under control they heard a noise in the distant. She was off as fast as ever. Her energy had been building up and now it was being released. Ratty and the rest try as they might; to keep up with her were left behind.

As Ruddy approached the noise she hid behind the vegetation, looking out to see what it was. A white dog with a black patch over its eye was barking and rolling around a hedgehog. This was not something the Mouhumes liked. Hedgehogs could kill a Mouhume with their sharp prickly spines. The Mouhumes could do nothing with a hedgehog so they kept away when possible.

The dog was rolling the hedgehog around the grass, hitting it with his paw and yelping as he did so, one or two spikes were in his face. The dog moved the hedgehog near to the hedge then the hedgehog unrolled and went on its way. The dog, covered in blood from his paw and face, was lying on the grass rubbing his face trying to get the quills out but each time pushing them in deeper.

Ruddy was memorized by this. The dog was as round as a barrel a strong looking muscular beast. It was whining. She crept towards the dog from behind, the only experience the Mouhumes had with dogs had not been pleasant.

She jumped onto the back of his neck. The dog froze. Then Ruddy, holding on to the dog's fur, bent down towards the side of the dog's face and started to pull out the spines. The dog was still not moving as she pulled out another one. She then leant towards the other side and pulled the last one from his face. The dog then rolled over onto his side and lifted his paw up as if to show that he had a quill in his pad. Ruddy looked at his pad then pulled hard to get it out.

Ruddy had no sooner done this, when she heard a noise from the top of the garden. Another dog similar to this one but with different colours was barking. This was a female dog; she came running down the garden towards Ruddy with bad intentions on her face.

The white dog jumped up head butting the other dog knocking the wind out of her, knocking her over. Then he stood over her as if he was telling her something. The dark colour dog got to her feet then ran towards Ruddy. Her face expression now changed. She had mischief on her face but not in a bad way, more playful.

Her head went down and her front legs pouncing on the ground. She began jumping from side to side. Her rear end was up and her tail was wagging. She wanted to play. Ruddy walked towards the dog, rubbing the dog's face. Then the dog licked Ruddy: its wet slavery tongue was licking Ruddy from her feet to the top of her head covering her with saliva. She was soaking wet

Ratty and the others were now hiding in the vegetation. They had not seen everything that had happened but sufficiently made up their minds that she was something of a marvel. No other Mouhume had ever made contact with any type of creature, yet to be licked with affection was an achievement. They were amazed and amused by what they were seeing but they needed to move on. Suddenly, a voice from the house was calling the dogs.
"Buster, Tilly come in."

The Mouhumes journey

The dogs stopped what they were doing and ran up towards the house wagging their tails with affection for the voice calling for them. As they got nearer to the house the white dog called Buster turned and looked down the garden. His body language and the look in his eye, was full of gratitude as if to say thank you.

Tilly, as always, was playful with her owner. She barked and jumped around with fondness and with misbehaviour in her eyes. If you never knew the dog you would be a bit apprehensive but her owner knew it was just Tilly's way for attention. Her chest was like a barrel. Buster was bigger in build but just the same as Tilly with his playful ways. When his owner came in from work he would take her shoes and run off with them just for a chase.

The two dogs were of similar age. Buster was a year older. Not that you could tell. They would walk for hours and when they got back they would still run around the house. Kez lived with her father who was away most the time with her brother. They worked all over the world. Her father was the owner of Buster and her brother the owner of Tilly. The dogs were both English bull terriers. Kez liked the company of the dogs and often had Tilly when her brother was away but when he was back he would take Tilly back. It was always just a short time that he was back so that was not too bad and he would be around most Sundays for lunch. Kez was okay with this as she had as much energy as them so they were well matched.

Once again the Mouhumes had to move on. They moved as it turned out, about two gardens higher. It was a big garden with a large shed, a large greenhouse then another smaller shed just behind them.

Chapter 4
Out of Sight

IT WAS GETTING lighter now so they would be better off hiding with some sort of shelter over them. They could hear running water from the top of the garden. One of the Mouhumes scaled up the side of the shed. High enough to see where the sound of running water was coming from he told the others that it was at the top part of the garden. The pond was nearly as big and as wide as the garden with a bridge going over it.

But now they would have to hide as they could hear the human cars starting up, doors being shut, humans talking and plates being scraped in gardens nearby. It was as if all the humans woke up at the same time. The Mouhumes could now be in danger of being seen so they would have to move in and around the shrubbery. This was something they could do easily. They hurried. There was plenty of room under the two sheds, plenty of buckets and plant pots lying around that would give them cover if needed.

There was around ten or so under the smaller shed and the rest under the larger shed which was nearly as twice the size as the smaller shed. One or two of the Mouhumes under the smaller shed noticed a hole in the floor, so they climbed up to see what was in the shed.

It was a right mess. There were tables, chairs and even an old lawn mower. There were also tools of all types: some for the garden and some for other things. None looked as if they had been used for a long time and everything seemed like it had been put away in a hurry. Things were piled on top of each other but for a Mouhume it was okay as there were plenty of hiding places.

It turned out to be a sunny day. There was not a lot of cloud, like it had been over the last few weeks. Now they were in a human region: a dangerous place they had no idea about so they would have to make do with where they were until darkness came and then they could move on.

The leaders, who had gathered under the larger shed, they were talking about what they should do. Should they send two or three teams out in different directions to save time later in order to see which way they should go and which place would be better? Or should they wait until all the others had returned as a number had gone out looking for food once they had decided they would stay under the shed during daylight.

A group of Mouhumes who went in search of food once things had gone quiet after a short time the noise returned. The humans were back but this time from what they could see they had some that were younger and smaller.

The Mouhumes watched as some of the younger humans went into a big motor vehicle, this had lots of windows. They could hardly believe what they were seeing. Humans were going into these things. The Mouhumes could see them sitting: some quiet, some clearly finding it unsettling and some were laughing and were jumping from one place to another. The older humans were waving their hands then walked off as the motor vehicle drove away. It was a strange place to say the least.

Once again it went quiet, hardly a human to be seen. The Mouhumes, who had been watching, could now go back and report what they had seen.

The Mouhumes leaders wondered if this was a daily ritual but one thing they had no doubt about was, they must leave as soon as possible. They would send small teams out to find a way out and to find food. They knew the pond near the house would provide them with water.

They got five sets of two to go and explore the area. It might be the right time in daylight and smaller groups would hardly be seen by any potential enemies. At night time other dangers would show themselves. At least in daylight they could see a good distance ahead this would help avoid any possible danger.

So five groups of two Mouhumes went on their way, they knew what they had to do and the areas they had to go. Tube, the leader, simply spread his fingers out onto the dry ground under the shed and the groups had to go in that direction. Those left behind knew which group went in which direction: the small finger was two experienced Mouhumes, those who went in the direction of the thumb were also experienced Mouhumes, the ones that went in direction of the index finger would also be experienced, those who went in the direction of the middle finger were likely to be the least experienced and those on the ring finger were there to help, if and when needed.

Off they went, spread out and hidden away. It was a journey they needed to do, they left with their little bags of food, water and a time they had been given to go as far as they could, taking in everything they possibly could then to return and report back.

They went through gardens and open fields that the humans had used, the Mouhumes knew this by the tell tale signs. If there were any obstacles in their way they would have to change direction slightly, so the Mouhumes would often leave a sign, a broken twig, a scuff on the ground, not always the best sign, however, it was still a sign of sorts, it was better than none at all. Especially if they ever got lost and a rescue party would be needed to come look for them,

When they reached the end of their time, they found themselves still in the large housing estate, it was never ending. Some gardens were better than others. Some just had a lawn: that was no good for the Mouhumes an open space like that would be fatal.

It had been quiet but for some reason the humans started to appear again. Cars were pulling up with children and parents coming home. It was not as busy as the morning time but there were still too many humans arriving. It was lunchtime; some children were coming back home for lunch as well as some of the adults. It was nothing like it had been in the morning and nothing like it would be later that evening.

Time was up they headed back to the others, back towards the two large sheds. Back to where they realised was the most secure place they had found as most the other gardens had little, if anything, to hide under. In the distance all they could see were more and more houses.

When they arrived back to the sheds they reported what they had seen while on their journey both the good and the bad. They explained that they had taken a little longer to return than expected but that was due to the fact that it was now lunchtime and humans were back around the houses and they had to hide and keep out of sight, they reported everything back.

Tube trusted the judgment of those he had sent out. He had kept Ruddy back, as she, more than any needed to rest. Tube knew if they were to stand any chance, he needed her at full strength. He was right to do so; she slept most of the time the trackers had been out.

Outside it had gone quiet again. They knew they would be safer staying another night, they would all rest and tomorrow they would send another team out in other directions to see what if any way they could go. In no time at all, in the smaller shed, they had all the space cleared and hiding areas created to keep them safe. Under the big shed they noticed pieces of wood and all sorts of other things that they would be able to make use of.

This was only going to be a short stop. This was not going to be a permanent place. They knew what they had in their old home and that's what they wanted back. A place away from humans and any danger humans brought with them. They wanted a place on top of a hill with woodland around them so they could see from the tree tops as far away as possible. They wanted to be able to see if human machines were heading towards them to give them a chance to escape, not like what had happened to them before. It was sudden and it wiped most of them out, killing some and those who had been lucky enough to flee were now spilt into areas that they had never visited before.

The Mouhumes were in a world they had no idea about. It seemed that they might be stuck. If they went back the way they came, the dangers could be even greater so they needed to find a way out of this human pack and move on. They started to settle down and rest.

Soon they knew they would have to go out gathering food. What kind of food would they find? They had seen humans putting food out on, what they could only call high platforms, for the birds. Did the humans worship the birds? A large number of houses had these raised areas. Birds and Mouhumes did not get on that well. Equally wanting the same food and often ended up in a fight. Depending on which type of bird, the Mouhumes often had to take a step back.

It was nothing they had not encountered before. There were one or two Mouhumes who were good climbers but even they had problems with most of these bird tables because the platform was normally over a post. They might have been able to climb the post, but at the top they had no way of getting onto the platform.

During the night before they settled down, one or two of the Mouhumes had a look around the area. The garden next to them had lots of little houses, almost if not better, than the human houses around them. There were different in styles, and each one looked as if they had been constructed for some creature not much different in size to the

Mouhumes. They mentioned this to one of the older Mouhumes but received no response.

The elder Mouhume had then reported this to the Mouhumes leaders. They all agreed that they would have to be on their guard, so that night they had more than the normal number of guards on watch. The night passed without any misfortune. Different types of animals had come their way but nothing amiss. Even one or two creatures they had not seen before had passed through and some they were only too aware of. On the whole, it was a quiet night.

The next day came. There was a lot of noise again and it lasted for a good while. The dry ground under the shed where Tube the day earlier, had pressed his hand to create the directions for them to go, could still be seen. Tube now wiped it clear with his foot so he could use it for today's directions, even though they knew which way they had already gone the day before.

They had a number of ways to show other Mouhumes which way they had gone, that only a Mouhume would know, something as simple as putting or turning a leaf: even better if there were a large number of leaves lying on the ground. A Mouhume would see the difference almost straight away and know which way to go.

The Mouhumes had experience along with great fighting skills. The younger Mouhumes would have to learn from the older ones and learn quickly. They knew that with these strange times and new experiences, they would always have to be quick thinking and have fast reflexes. Normally there would always be at least a third of the community resting enabling these skills to remain sharp.

The noise started to dim. The humans, just like the day before thinned out, they were going about their way and just like the day before they would return later that evening. This was the time the Mouhumes would have to be out of sight.

The next squad, who were going out to find a new and hopefully a safe area so that they could make a new home, as those the day before were given their directions, food and whatever else they needed. A small little pouch was tied around each of their waists: a bladder, no bigger than a Mouhume's fist that once belonged to some poor creature that had met their misfortune, was now used as a water carrier.

This time Tube only sent four pairs of scouts. The time came for him to place his hand in the dry earth to direct them. His fingers were closer than the day before and they were told how far they must go and the time they had to do it in. The time was a little longer than the day before.

As always they had to make a decision after reporting back, whether it was going to be worth the journey for the others? A heavy burden for any to make, that was why Tube would listen to each and every Mouhume individually who made it back.

It was like a military operation with speed and agility. They had gone in and out of hedges and undergrowth. In no time at all they had gone through a number of gardens then they came to the beginning of woodland.

First they had to get through the fence that was separating the last garden to the woodland. It was easy enough: a wired fence with holes in it as big as tennis balls. They had not got far when a smell of rotten flesh was in the air. They would have to go and inspect what it was.

The sight that greeted them was breathtaking. They were shocked this was something they had never seen before. Black bin bags were ripped open: parts of birds in one and the other had parts of rabbits. Rats were ripping into the bags taking out the rotten bodies.

Suddenly another bag was thrown over from one of the gardens. They heard a human laughing; another bag was thrown over, ripping open as it landed on to the thorn bush. No sooner had the human gone when hundreds of rats came out from the undergrowth. It was a terrible sight to see and no way could they go that way. The Mouhumes would be killed!

The scouts had the sense to remain far enough away when this feeding frenzy was going on; the dead animals had caused a distraction. Quickly they turned and hurried back leaving no trace that they had been there. If the rats had not been so intense with what they were doing then the Mouhumes would have been slaughtered, there was no doubt about that.

They headed back, taking a different route so that if they had been seen they would not lead any enemy straight back to where they were based.

This took them back in the direction they had first come days earlier. The same direction but to a different area, it was five or so gardens apart, a big enough area for it to be new and undiscovered. They gathered back together. They were all shaken, shocked and bewildered about the events they had just seen. None of the group had the experience to deal with what they had seen.

They had forgotten to leave signals for any Mouhume that might come looking for them, but under the circumstances they could be forgiven. Each of them held on to their weapons, one had a nail and one or two had the spines from the hedgehog that they encountered days before. They split up again so they would be harder to detect, but they kept in sight of each other.

They moved in and out of the gardens with speed and agility but not the same mindset as they had only a short time before. This time it was a matter of life or death and the determination each one had, it was going to be life first before death.

The scouts had recovered their directions. They were back on the track they had came through days earlier there were still one or two directions that had been left days earlier by those who had been in front. A little mark here and a twig there, only a Mouhume would know the signs. This put them at rest to a certain degree, at least now they knew they were not that far from the shed.

As they approached the garden they were greeted by those who were on the lookout. One or two led them to Tube; he was in the smaller shed with the hole in the floor. They were working on defences so that if they had an attack they could prevent anything getting into the shed of a similar size.

They knew the drill: not to talk to anyone about what they had seen, good or bad. Tube had to be the first to know and sometimes one or two of the Mouhumes that were high up in the leadership, but that was only when Tube needed another opinion, only when he was unsure what they should do for the best.

Tube came as they sat down eating and drinking. Tube knew by the expression on each of their faces that things had not gone too well. Tube called some of the other Mouhumes over to listen. Carefully they listened as they got the reports back from each Mouhume who had been on that expedition.

By the time they listened to the last one they knew that danger was not far away and in great numbers. Ratty who had sat listening knew by the numbers they had the Mouhumes would not stand a chance. They would be killed and eaten.

The talks went late into the early hours of the next day. What should they do? Try somewhere else? Go back to the warren and join forces with Rug?

The decision was too much for any of them. It would have to be a vote and if split, it would make one side even more vulnerable. As they were talking about the possibilities, some of the Mouhumes continued digging under the large shed they were getting a good way down. In their minds it was going to be for a short time but for now they needed somewhere for safety, at least until they knew what they were going to do.

Chapter 5
Indecisive Tactics

TUBE AND RATTY sent the word around for all the Mouhumes to gather under the larger of the two sheds. There was far more of them than Tube had first thought so some ended up under the other shed as well.

They were told what the scouts had seen the day before, Tube told them all about the human and the dead animal remains, then they were told about the number of rats that arrived to eat the remains.

There was a lot of talking then suddenly a voice, from the middle of the crowd, Joy, spoke up and asked why they could not stay here: food was ample and some had already started to make living accommodation under the sheds.

Others were still talking amongst themselves; no-one could clearly hear what was being said, some were agreeing and others wanted to move on to find a place out of sight from the humans who seemed to murder creatures on mass numbers then feed them to rats. Who were even more dangerous in large numbers.

Rats had always been around, never too far away from any food source but the Mouhumes had never seen this amount. The discussions lasted a long time, in the end they all agreed they had to make it as safe as possible while they were there.

Everyone left and went back to what ever they were doing before their meeting; those who had been hunting for food went on their way whilst other Mouhumes went to rest or continue making their accommodation comfortable and secure.

Meanwhile Tube and Ratty were discussing the next group of scouts this time. Tube and Ratty were going too.

Ratty started to pick those who he wanted. They only needed six more to make eight in total. Happy with those he picked, he knew they were strong, fast, had agility and between them they could cover a large area in little time, as there was only one more area they had not explored they needed to be experienced Mouhumes.

The Mouhumes journey

It would be later that night when the streets went silent. It still had danger but no different to what they were used to in the field they had moved from.

As the rest of the Mouhumes went about their business Tube and Ratty and the others went on their way to discover what ever lay ahead, wonderful lands, they hoped.

Woozy, back in camp, was looking around the next door's garden at the magnificent model houses they were big enough for a Mouhume to go in. He had seen nothing like it, he wondered if the human who lived in the house built these and if so why?

Inside were rooms, these were not just models these were homes for something small like a Mouhume, but what? Woozy looked around, he sensed something was watching him, he turned around quickly, nothing was there feeling uneasy he left in a hurry.

Back under the shed some of the Mouhumes had started to dig into the dry earth. In no time at all they reached clay. This was met with mixed feelings. It was hard for them to dig through clay. They had gone through a lot in a short time and digging clay used up a lot of energy. They had never worked so hard but they needed it to be safe and underground would be the best place to be. Linden was helping to dig out the earth under the shed. They had done a lot. Most of the Mouhumes could live there now if needed. This was good practise as if and when they moved on because no matter where they moved to, under the ground was nearly all the same and they could shape it as they needed it to be.

Ruddy was out and about. She had not been asked to go on the scouting expedition. She was doing her own exploring. Five gardens up next to a big grassed area with a path leading down. She hid in amongst some plants, watching humans walking up and down. She was trying to understand them: how they talked, what they were doing, where they were going, what was in the bags? There was so much going on in her head, she needed to know.

The garden she was in had beetroot growing. She had never had beetroot before and she was feeling a little hungry so she bit into the beetroot still in the ground. It was firm but not what she had expected, it was not dry or juicy but just right. In no time at all she had nearly eaten all of what was shown above the soil.

She had never felt so good. The beetroot made her feel different. The nutrients in the beetroot, was something the Mouhumes had never had before. She would have to go and tell the rest of the Mouhumes how good she felt and they would have to dig up this wonderful plant. As she approached the camp the look on some of the Mouhumes faces was of shock, one or two even ran away.

What was going on? She turned around quickly to see if there was something behind her. Why were some of the Mouhumes running away? Then she was surrounded by a number of Mouhumes.

All they could see was that Ruddy was covered in a red and purple colouring; it was all over her mouth and her hands. They wondered if she had she been attacked but by what? This was not blood from a Mouhume, What had she done?

She pulled a chunk of beetroot out from her pouch and bit into it. To those watching it was as if she was biting into a lump of flesh. She then passed it onto a younger Mouhume who then took a bite.

It was as if the goodness from the plant was absorbed almost straight away by the Mouhumes body. It was something the Mouhumes had been missing and needed.

They all had a taste. The goodness from the beetroot worked: helping to feed them and gave them the nutrition that they needed to help with healing. The only downside was that they were covered in the purple juice making them look frightening because they had a reddish purple colouring around their mouths.

The next thing they did was to collect as many beetroots as they could. The gardener lost half of his crop.

Once back, they had to get cleaned up, luckily for them there was plenty of water at the back of the shed. There were three water barrels and one had a tap, the Mouhumes worked out how to turn it on and off, ideal to help get them clean.

***

Meanwhile Tube and Ratty had reached as far as they would go. They had travelled fast and now it was time to rest. They sat under a bush that had gone out of control but provided good cover for them. There they took out their little bags of food.

Looking around while sitting down, the Mouhumes took in the surrounding area. It was nowhere that a Mouhume could or would want to live. It had been a place where humans had once lived but now it was rubble. Houses were half pulled down, machines pushed and pulled at the bricks and there was a dusty smell in the air from the machines.

Tube realised that all the areas had been checked, they had travelled as far as they could go without having to stay in a makeshift shelter. Tube thought about doing that but as always that would have to be a decision made by all the Mouhumes.

After they rested for a short time they were ready to go back. Ratty said that they should go back in a slightly different way. Tube was unsure but as usual Ratty persuaded Tube. He could put up a good argument: the path they would go back along Ratty wanted to go on the right side going back and he convinced Tube to go on the left side but in sight of each, there would be four in each group.

This would give them a better idea of what was around the area and if it looked promising they could quickly look it over. It made sense, a wider area was being explored but Tube's worry was that if they got into danger would the others see and be able to help?

In no time at all they were back in the gardens belonging to humans. Some gardens they had not been in so this might be beneficial to them discovering more about the surrounding area. Tube did not want to stay any longer than needed. He had plans to move on once they all had a day or two of resting and collecting food.

They finally approached the path they had previously come on. It had been a disappointing mission. There was nothing at all to show for it. So when Tube and Ratty and the other explorers came back in just a short time, the change was astonishing. As they approached the camp, to there surprise it had changed, the work that had been done was amazing.

The goodness from the beetroot had given the Mouhumes something they never had. It gave them energy as it released its nutrition into the little bodies.

Something they had needed but never had. Some who had been under the weather had also tried it and seemed better.

Tube and Ratty went around the new camp. It was almost finished. If they had not been intending to move on, it would be as good as they could possibly want but they felt that they must still go and find a safer place. But this would be a good place. Safety and defensive devices had been put in place so as a short term solution it would do.

Tube and Ratty were given some beetroot and almost immediately they felt the benefits. The beetroot had worked like nothing they had before, it was like magic. The nourishment they had been missing was in this one plant.

It was getting dark now and they needed to sort a few things out. They needed to arrange who was doing what tasks the next day? What they needed to do and how far would the next group of scouts go? All of these things would have to be talked about.

Chapter 6
Next Door

EARLY THE NEXT morning Ruddy was doing what she done best and that was exploring and getting herself into trouble. She thought that something in the next garden had been watching her but she could not see what it was. Every time she turned around, no matter how fast, there was nothing there.

She was determined to find out what it was. Some of the other Mouhumes were waking up as she went out with her hunting weapons. One of the younger Mouhumes saw this and sneaked behind her, following her from a distance.

Ruddy was fast and almost in stealth mode. She was through the hedge that parted the two gardens in a flash. She looked around at the different plants and the life-like ornaments of animals and houses. She thought the houses looked as real as the human houses. Yes she thought, they were small enough for something similar in size to live in.

She had been in one of the houses a day earlier but now she was on the hunt to see what might live in there. Ruddy would find out one way or another. She drew out her sharp thorn and she held it in her mouth so that her hands were still free. If needed, she could scale up or down the plants.

As she entered the little house she was astonished how big it seemed inside. It was hollow but the ground went down some 12 inches or so. She jumped to the bottom to see if there were any holes or tunnels leading off.

Nothing, empty, all she could see was a deep hole with a model house above it. She looked up at the roof of the house. A little light was coming in through the doorway she had entered. One or two cracks in the sides and roof were also letting in light.

It took a little time for her eyes to adjust to the difference in light from outside. She stood in the middle turning around and looking from side to side. Nothing seemed out of place. She could not sense anything that might be harmful.

Then suddenly, she knew she was not alone. She jumped up the side of the hole, heading towards the doorway and reached out, grabbing a hold of whatever it was hiding at the side of outside wall. She then flung it on the floor and jumped onto it with her thorn, just stopping at the side of the Young Mouhumes neck.

The young Mouhume had followed her. He had almost lost his life. There were not many Mouhumes who could have stopped in that situation. It would be kill or be killed. A split moment, a slight hesitation has cost many a Mouhume their life.

Fortunately for the young Mouhume it was Ruddy. She was the fastest and most skilful of the Mouhumes. That was exactly what all the young Mouhumes had talked about. Not the leaders, like Ratty or Tube but Ruddy.

Ruddy picked up the young Mouhume and slapped his head with the back of her hand. No words were said as Ruddy had already realised that something else was close by and she knew this time it was not a Mouhume.

She pulled the young Mouhume up by the scruff of his neck and put him in the ornamental house she had just come out of.

He hid behind the doorway knowing that something was going to happen, scared for his life and for Ruddy he kept still. In the meantime, Ruddy was climbing up one of the tall plants. Where she would get a better view of what was around her.

Nothing seemed to be obviously wrong. The birds were still on different plants picking insects off. They would normally be the first to be off if danger was around. So what could it be? Even she could not understand, but her senses were never wrong.

She jumped back to the ground and headed back to where the young Mouhume was so she could get him out of the way. This was not somewhere she wanted to be, especially with a young inexperienced Mouhume.

As she approached the little house she suddenly turned around and jumped on whatever it was. She held on to it and was just about to strike it when she was lifted up into the air. Whatever they were she had two holding onto her, one was still on the ground as she looked down to see what she was up against.

It was something she had never seen before. Its body was similar size to hers but it had wings like a dragonfly. That was it, it was a giant dragonfly. By now she was high in the sky then suddenly she felt herself being let go. She spun towards the earth knowing that she would die. There was nothing she could do.

The young Mouhume on the ground, with fear in his eyes saw what was happening. This was Ruddy, the bravest Mouhume ever! Now he was going to see her end, not in any battle they had encountered before. Yes she had fought birds that had tried similar things, picking up and dropping the enemy from the sky.

Ruddy was heading towards the earth with speed. Now her back would smash onto the ground. She could not turn around. She stopped trying and accepted her fate. Allsorts was going through her head. It seemed to last forever.

There was not a thud as you would expect but a gentle landing. The thing that she had attacked earlier had now swooped up and with precision timing saved Ruddy. Ruddy's weight knocked the wind out of this thing and they crashed landed onto the earth both rolling into a heap.

Ruddy was first up, dazed and unsteady on her feet. The two others who had dropped her landed beside them then jumped onto Ruddy pinning her down and knocking her weapon out of reach.

The young Mouhume saw this so he started to run towards them, he ran straight into a fist knocking him head over heels. He rolled then jumped to his feet as he seen Ruddy do. His legs were trembling with fear and his head was still in a daze from the blow to his head. Before he knew it he was also took to the ground with one of these creatures on top of him, who was laughing at the same time at how easy it was to take them down.

Ruddy, trying hard to get up, was unable to do so. She had never felt so useless in all her conflicts. She closed her eyes knowing that she had met her match and now she believed she was going to meet her end just like she had taken so many lives before.

But instead she was picked up. It was not that different to how she had picked up the young Mouhume not that long before. The creature that broke her fall had, this time, picked himself up. The two who had took

Ruddy for a flight stood in close proximity watching for anymore violent behaviour.

Ruddy looked at this creature and tried to work out what it was. Then it started to talk to Ruddy. To Ruddy's surprise she could understand what was being said.

It turned out he had been watching the Mouhumes from a distance and had seen how Ruddy was fearless. Her speed and her agility was something he had not seen before in any other living thing and curiosity had got the better of him.

They had been watching all the time but not letting themselves be seen. They could blend into any surroundings. Ruddy had the ability and skill to know that something was nearby and grab hold of one. That in itself was something they had rarely come across.

But their ability was better than any Mouhume would ever be. They were not as aggressive as the Mouhumes but they could defend themselves.

They told Ruddy the humans call them fairies and they could understand all living creatures, not that they got on with them all. They had their enemies, just as all living things did. As much as they tried to get along with everyone, sometimes this was mistaken for weakness.

As this was being explained to Ruddy the young Mouhume had gotten away to get help for Ruddy. In no time at all there was a number of Mouhumes ready to fight for Ruddy. This would not happen for any Mouhume but Ruddy had saved so many, they needed to try and save her.

They got themselves into position ready to attack. After all there was only three they could see and they didn't look very strong. Before anyone could say anything the young Mouhume went to attack the fairy that had punched him in the face earlier.

In no time at all Ruddy was back to her feet. She stood between the fairy and the Mouhume and the other Mouhumes stopped in there tracks. Ruddy called for them to stop. This was something she had never experienced before.

Dropping from a great height she was certainly at death's door and there was nothing she could have done to avoid her end but for this fairy.

Without doing what he had done for her, her fortune would have been sealed.

She also knew the Mouhumes had the disadvantage. The fairies had speed, wing power and strength and maybe more skills in hiding, ready to come out and attack or defend.

Her knowledge and instinct knew they would be better friends than enemies. The Mouhumes stood down but would be ready for a full on attack if needed, watching for any sudden or aggressive movements.

Ratty stood near Ruddy and looked at her in a way as if to say was she all right? Without saying a word Ruddy knew what he wanted to know.

Her eyes told him what he needed to know but even behind her assurance her eyes, when Ratty looked deeper, not even Ruddy could conceal her fear.

After a short time the fairy that had been attacked by Ruddy came forward and told Ratty they had unfortunately met during a moment of madness and all they wanted was to make acquaintances.

The Fairy told them that he had not intended to startle Ruddy, who in turn had attacked him, knocking him to the ground. His friends had to save him and the only way they knew was to get her into the air. They had seen her fight and knew this was their only chance.

Saying this took nothing away from Ruddy's fighting skill. Her respectability was still intact but to her she knew that she had no chance. She was as weak as a baby and would have been easy killed if not for the mercy of the fairy.

Her confidence had been dented. She had faced death many times and never thought anything of it but what had just happened had her self-esteem at an all time low. She could hear the younger Mouhumes talking about it and how she had, once again, escaped death.

They headed back to camp. There was going to be a big discussion and the heads of the Mouhumes would have to seriously consider if they should move now.

Ruddy went to a part of the camp to be by herself. She had to get her head around this. This was something she found hard. Some other creature saving her, never in all her days had this been done.

Mousey came to talk to her, she told him her concerns. He listened then asked her if she had ever shown mercy. She looked up at him and shook her head. He asked again, once again she shook her head. Mousey asked Ruddy about the dog that had thorns in his face and pads, she looked at him without any expression on her face.
"Was that not kindness? Pity, you could have left it be, you had no idea what it would do if it had bad intentions. I must admit it doesn't happen often, more so when it had just been attacked."

Ruddy jumped to her feet and agreed, the meeting was about to start and she needed to talk to Tube and the other elders before it was opened up to all the Mouhumes after all the meeting was about whether they would go or stay.

The talks, once again, lasted almost all night. Would the fairies be friends or would they take advantage when they found out if they had any weakness?

Chapter 7
Next Day

EARLY THE NEXT morning one or two of the Mouhumes were already up and going about their business: some were on food mission whilst others were scouting the area.

Tube was with Mousey. Mousey was explaining to him that Ruddy was concerned about what had happened to her and her confidence was knocked.

Ratty walked into the area where they were talking. It was part of a chamber some of the Mouhumes had made the day before. It was not that big, five or six Mouhumes would be comfortable in there.

It was not that long into their conversation when word got to them that Ruddy was up and about. Tube sent Mousey to go and ask her to come to where they were talking as he needed to talk to her in the light of day.

Mousey went to find her, when he found her she was sitting near the rhubarb plant at the back of the shed. The rhubarb was just starting to ripen. The big leaves were hiding her from any danger that might come from the sky.

She was still looking sad. She could not work out why she was feeling like this. Mousey tried to comfort her but she was having none of it.

She decided to go and see Tube and Ratty to see if they could help her with their wisdom but even they could not work it out. After another long talk it was Mousey who came up with the idea that Ruddy should go and find the fairy who had saved her and ask why?

She was ever so confused. As she went into the garden next door she had a good look around and took notice. It was like a smaller version of a human village. There was an odd house here, a bungalow there and at least three in the garden near the main house.

Suddenly something took hold of her arm; it was the fairy from the day before. She jumped but held back her normal instinct which would be to attack. The fairy beckoned her to follow him. There was a large hedge that Ruddy had not taken any notice of before. It blended in with the rest of the garden, there was no reason to take notice of it; it was nothing out of the ordinary.

But as she was taken through the hedge she became fully aware of what she was being shown: at least a quarter of that garden was a small village. How did none of the Mouhumes see this when they were exploring the area and how did she miss this?

There were about twenty miniature houses. They were big enough for the fairies or even the Mouhumes. So how had she missed seeing this? Something this big! She was now being led down what could only be described as a street. Houses on both sides made to look like what humans lived in.

Her head now was full of questions. How did the human of this garden not see this? How did they not interfere? How could they be next to humans and never be discovered.

She was then taken into a doorway that led down a passageway and then out again into a clearing. This was nothing like what she had just seen; this was far more than what she had ever seen before. This was nothing that she could have prepared herself for. Her head, already doing overtime and was now about to be blown away. It was too much to take in that she passed out.

Mousey was going to follow her just to make sure that she was alright but got distracted by something. So when he picked up her trail, or what he thought was her trail, it did not take him long to work out that it was from the day before.

Ruddy had not left a trail today for some reason. Not that this was unusual. A Mouhume did not have to leave a trail so near where they had a camp but really should when they were entering some strange area.

Mousey took some time looking around the garden next door but could not find anything to tell him where she might be.

She maybe changed her mind and went off somewhere else to clear her mind. After all she had been under a lot of strain. Yes that would be it Mousy thought but he would still have to go and report back to the leaders Tube and Ratty just so they knew what was happening.

As Mousey approached, Tube and Ratty were in the distance talking to another Mouhume or telling him off. They were round the back of the two sheds in a little clearing. All sorts of plants were growing so there was plenty of overhead cover.

Mousey approached Tube but was silent as Tube's hand was raised in away that Mousey knew that he had to wait and stand quietly, which he did by the corner of the greenhouse.

There was nothing worse than being reprimanded and knowing others were watching. He knew he might also be getting the same in a short time for losing sight of Ruddy.

If she was in danger he would be in the deepest trouble as he was the one who said that he was more than capable to look out for her and he had also talked Ruddy into going to see the fairy who had saved her.

Ratty came towards Tube looking very angry he started to talk to him just out of earshot of Mousey. This was so Mousey could not hear what was being said. Ratty might have looked angry but Tube looked at ease. Mousey tried to get closer to hear what had upset Ratty but dared not get into the eyesight of one of them.

Ratty had now finished talking to Tube and saw Mousey wandering closer towards them, he called Mousey over with a kind of a growl in his voice.

This made Mousey jump, he had thought that he had not been seen but Tube knew that he would try and get near to hear what was said. Tube knew Mousey so well that he always wanted to know what and who were saying what.

This was not a bad thing as he was a walking knowledge of information on just about anything. If he did not know, Tube knew that just by asking Mousey it would be enough for him to find a way to find out what was needed.

This was one of Mousey strengths. Finding out things was something that he had done from an early age. Being inquisitive was like second nature to him.

But this did puzzle him. How could Ruddy disappear? Not even a trail which was second nature to all the Mouhumes. Mousey reported what he had found, or in this case not found. He also explained what his next actions would be.

    Mousey's was going to talk to the young Mouhume who had seen the fight. He wanted to know from start to finish just what happened. This would or might help him to find Ruddy …

Chapter 8
Unrest at the Warren

HE WAS THE only one that would be the hero. Only he could lead the Mouhumes to safety and now it was his time. He had driven all those out who had once been leaders. He would now have to do more than drive out the one time leaders he would have to destroy them to put fear into any other Mouhumes who might think the role was up for the taking.

With the role he would have to have advisers and strong leadership. They might advise him but he would have the last say.

He had some big shoes to fill. Tube had been the leader for a long time and had some good followers and some fearless fighters at his side, one being Ruddy, Ruddy the living legend….

He should have killed her when she was weak and worn out he thought, he had heard the stories about her being almost dead then attacking and killing her enemies, therefore he dared not under estimate her.

If he had ordered her death and she was to take out one or more of those who tried to carry out her demise, even in her weak state. The rest of the Mouhumes would have killed those without hesitation.

He had done the right thing. He had tainted her reputation at a time she had little fight left in her, but he had no idea that she would still have a number of followers.

Now they were divided and open to allsorts. What was the way forward? In numbers they had fighters, strength and wisdom. Now they had more than halved. This was a new world, new danger's none of them had faced before. So not even Tube, with his experience and knowledge, would be any help.

Rug was standing with his followers looking out into the night sky wondering what his next move should be. He was feeling a bit fearful. If he had kept quiet he could have learned more from his elders.

It might have been new to all of them but their experience would have been useful. All he had around him was weakness and inexperience. Even his own fighting skills were no match for what lay ahead. He knew he had to find away to get back with those who had left but not to show any weakness by doing so.

The weather was improving; the humans were starting to use the park area again. Sometimes they dropped bits of food around the car park and on the grass areas after they had their picnic. It was not a safe place, he could sense this. As the weather got better more and more humans came around the area and it would be only a matter of time before they were found out.

The nights were getting lighter; the protection of darkness was disappearing. If they where to make a move it would have to be now and hopefully they would find some sort of trail, even after the weeks that had past. The likelihood of that would be almost impossible but the unrest in the warren was reaching danger point. The lack of food and the wildlife around that would kill them if they were found was more than Rug had ever known.

He summoned those who he had ordered to follow Ruddy when she left so that he could find the start of the trail. There were only around fifty of this group left. Some had died by poison left on food to kill vermin and others had met their end through other wildlife.

Some in the warren would not be strong enough to leave; their health had taken a turn for the worse. Rug had taken the decision now was the time to leave and hopefully if they were lucky enough to find Tube and any of others they might join and be as it used to.

Those who had followed Tube and Ruddy came to see Rug. Rug had learned to question them separately. Rug listened to what they had told him, he went deeper into certain parts so that he could get a picture of what danger lay ahead, what obstacles they would encounter.

It would appear that they had both lost sight of those who had left around the same time as there was a steep hill that they had to travel up. It was so steep that the two Mouhumes following them had gave up near the top but they did climb half way up a tree, near the top of the hill so that they could see what was beyond. It had been a dark night but what they had seen in the distance was nothing but more danger.

Rug had asked what sort of danger there might be. They both told the same tale, lights in the sky (street lights) lights that where moving (cars) noise in the distance nothing that they had heard before, (humans having fun).

They equally believed that they would meet their death heading that way. They waited a long time before they came back to the warren, so that they knew for certain that Ruddy and the others where not coming back that way.

Rug had asked why they had not reported back to him. They said that when they had returned there was mayhem. Some of those who went with Ruddy had taken food and had left little. They had no sooner returned to report what they had seen but were told to go and find food by some of the others.

Rug nodded and admitted that there had been panic. When they discovered that food had been taken, fear confusion and a number of other worries set in. The food supply was still no better. This was the main reason why they would have to move as soon as they could. They still needed to work out the best way forward.

Illness was taking its toll, numbers were dwindling, Tube had always said that the burrow was only going to be a short stop until they had rested and had enough food to take with them.

Tube and those who had been forced to go had to take some of the food supply. Not as much as they would have taken if not for the speedy exit but enough to keep them going until they found more. They had left what they considered to be sufficient for those left behind. After all they had been a community of friends and family for as long as they could remember.

Rug's thoughts drifted to those, who he had not seen after that morning when the earth had been dug and ripped apart in that moment. Many fled in different directions; some were even swallowed up by the earth as it turned.

He had seen, in that short time, so much death that he found it hard to rest or sleep. He was always on edge and always waiting for the next disaster. That's why he needed to be the leader. He did not want to be told what to do but the one telling the other Mouhumes as he had done on the morning with his quick thinking. He had saved a number of Mouhumes. Some had been killed by being told different things.

The fact of it was, it was either good fortune or bad luck. What had happened that day was awful for the Mouhumes community; big machines tore the earth apart. Some building development company had decided to build on the land. It had been undeveloped land that was no good for farming. Just land that no one wanted until now.

That's how the Mouhumes had never been disturbed. Once in a while they had encountered a human that was when someone had walked out of their way as it was not somewhere people would want to walk to. There was nothing there. The wildlife could go about their lives as normal.

Now Rug had to decide when they were leaving. He could see that it was pointless waiting any longer. Those who were poorly were not going to get any better. It was up to them if they wanted to attempt the next journey.

They waited until nightfall. It was not as dark as they would have liked but it was as dark as it was going to get. The food was shared out; each Mouhume would carry their own. Those who were staying would have food left for them.

There was around twenty or more Mouhumes going with Rug. At least another fifteen left in the warren who were old or injured and poorly. These and another twenty or so who wanted to stay to help those who were ill.

Rug felt bad about leaving them but over the past few weeks he had seen a number of deaths and illness due to the lack of food. So he decided he could not risk the rest of the Mouhumes in a place that was only going to kill them one way or another. It was going to be try or die journey and he decided to try the way that Tube had tried. If Tube and his followers had met their ends then there would be some sort of sign.

The hill was as steep as the scouts had said it was. That in its self was a hard task for some of the weaker Mouhumes but slowly they managed it. It took a lot longer than they thought it would. A number of trees up the hill give them cover so that they could rest awhile.

When they got to the top the road was empty. The street lights were on, giving them some idea what was in the distance. There were buildings, more than they had seen in the bottom of the park, lots more,

Rug thoughts were going crazy, more humans meant more danger but if Tube could make it through this he could.

They went through a number of gardens, not knowing they had missed the garden that Tube and the others had stopped at to rest the first night.

It was only two or three gardens away but far enough to miss the evidence that a Mouhume had stayed in that area. Rug had no idea how near he was to being on the same track as Tube. His heart and determination was starting to sink.

Rug was hoping that he could help those who were now with him and also hopeful that those who had left had found safety. He realised that he had been wrong trying to get rid of Ruddy, Rug should have known that she had a strong following.

It was not much longer when he decided that they should stop for a rest. He had pushed them harder than any other leader would have. They stopped just outside a garden in amongst some trees that ran alongside the gardens.

There was lots of undergrowth as well as dead bramble bushes. There was also a lot of new shoots just starting to grow. The thorns from the dead bushes would help to protect them from any over head danger.

The morning sunrise was just starting to light the sky. Now would be the time to establish what was around them, planning how to deal with it. It would also be a good time to try and find some food, but they had to keep out of the way from any danger that might be around.

Quickly they had made a little camp. It gave them protection from up above and from the sides unless it was big and strong and could break through the thorns

They started to eat the little food they had brought with them; they rested but only for a short time. Rug wanted to know what was around them and whether they could make use from anything. So he and two others went out into the woods to see what they could find.

They may have been undernourished and some in poor health but Rug had pushed them hard and fast. He had covered twice the distance that Tube had done. He had left the rest to eat what they had and so that they could recover their energy to be ready for the next move. Rug wanted to see which way they might go. He took two strong Mouhumes with him, both young and full of energy

In a little distance they came across a dead rat then another then more than he had ever seen before. It was like a battle field and then he came to the source. Black bin bags torn apart dead pigeon's half eaten. The smell was more than they could take, the three of them moved away as quickly as they could.

No matter how far they moved away from the devastation they still came across a dead rat, even other animals that had eaten the contaminated bodies.

Rug and his two companions settled down out of the way. One had recognised the smell, not the dead rotten corpse smell but something else in the air. He started to tell Rug that when they went to find Ruddy that they had came across something similar but Tube, in his wisdom, had said not to eat the food that was lying around no matter how hungry they were. Tube would not let anyone go near the food.

The Mouhume, telling the account, sunk his head. He told Rug how one Mouhume had gone back as they were all hungry, got a handful and ate it as he himself was going to do, but the Mouhume who had eaten the food fell to the ground dead. His eyes filled up. He could still see it, as if it was happing in front of him now. If it had been him, a moment earlier he also would be dead.

Rug could see that he was upset so he jumped to his feet. It was no good getting down in the dumps. He needed to lift morale. As the leader he believed himself to be and as he had seen so many times from Tube and Ratty, how they lifted the moral. Rug said without hesitation that they had learned something important and they should share this with the rest of their group.

He nodded to them and off he went to explore. They still, had not found any trace that Tube or any other Mouhume might have been in that area. It was frustration for him; he had hoped so much that he would have found something by now.

They had not travelled very far when they came to the gardens of humans. He scratched his head. They would not have gone anywhere near humans. He shook his head No what a silly idea!

It was time to head back to the others but first he wanted to find some food, then suddenly something took his attention. Birds were flying to the ground eating something left on the lawn; it looked like big lumps of food had been thrown out for the birds.

They all looked healthy enough. None were falling down dead. Would he risk it and take some food? As he considered this the other two Mouhumes ran towards the birds shouting and screaming arms waving in the air so that the birds flew away.

Rug was not far behind the other two, all of them grabbing handfuls of food then, just as fast they ran back into the woods and under the undergrowth their hearts beating so fast with excitement.

Now was the test! Would they dare eat it after seeing the mass of dead animals not that far away? They sniffed the food, nothing out of the ordinary. Not that they knew how bread would smell. Rug looked at the Mouhume, who had told him about the poison food, was the smell the same?

As they sat they watched the birds going back for the remainder of the food that was left on the lawn. They continued to watch the birds again. The birds ate every scrap of food that was on the lawn and still none fell down dead.

Rug tried a bit of bread the other two started to eat theirs as well. It was nothing that they had tried before so they had no idea what it should taste like. It seemed to fill the spot. That's all they wanted, to get rid of that hunger.

Lucky for them they were big chunks of bread, so they did not have to try to find anymore food. The bread was not that heavy to carry. All they had to do now was to go back and find those they had left behind.

With each one of them carrying two bits of food each it took them longer than they wanted. When they arrived back to the others, it was worth it, seeing the expression on their faces, joy and hopefulness. With what had seemed to be a death sentence back at the warren, there was now hope.

They stayed there the best part of that day. Only now and again they popped out in the nearby area to see what was around them. Plenty of birds and rabbits were around, now and again the odd human with dogs some off their leads.

There was plenty undergrowth for them to hide in. There was also the smells from the plants and the dampness in the air this all helped to hide their aroma.

One of the Mouhumes who had been with Rug was wearing an old crisp packed. When he was running across the garden lawn he must have just looked like an empty packet blowing in the wind.

Rug with his bits of cloth would also have looked like something blowing in the wind. The only one that might have looked like an animal was the third one. He was wearing bits of mouse skins put together to keep him warm. Now was the time they had to blend in with the human's world and use anything to help them, even things they may never have normally come into contact with, things like the crisp packet.

Rug once again sat with his thoughts. Tube was right to want to move away from the warren. There was not enough food around there. There might not be enough food here either but at least they had some to put away for the next day. They had eaten their fill for that day.

The daylight had seemed to last longer than normal, or it might have just been because they did not know the area and did not want too venture out of their camp.

Rug knew that they could not stay there for a long time. They would have to take it in turns to make trips out to discover what was around them.

Rug went out most times, only having a rest after every third outing. He was kept up to date with what they had seen on each occasion he had not gone with them.

Rug told them every time to look out for any sign that another Mouhume might have been there. He was desperate to find Tube and Ratty, Ruddy and all the others. He felt sick and upset that he had forced them to leave. Rug regretted it even more now that he too had made the decision to leave, especially after telling everyone that Tube was wrong when he had said that they would have to move on

The only difference was that he had told those he had left behind at the warren that he would be back with food and hopefully somewhere they could all be together and secure again.

Chapter 9
Alone at the Burrow

THOSE WHO WERE left at the burrow were not all sick and weak. Some had stayed to try and help the weak and ill to recover.

The weather was getting warmer. The sunlight was longer in the sky giving light for most of the day. The park area was getting fuller with more and more humans each day. This was not always a bad thing, as some would disregard food and drop it anywhere. Later that day, if the birds or other animals had not eaten it, the Mouhumes would scurry out of hiding holes and get it.

Food now was not becoming the issue as it was starting to mount up. They were storing it in the deepest part of the burrow in the darkest coolest part to help keep it as fresh for as long as they could. For now, those who were left had more than a sufficient amount of food. It would seem, those who had left due to there not being sufficient food was not a bad thing.

Those who had been too ill to travel were now getting stronger. Some had lost their lives but most had made it through. Numbers were picking up and with new baby Mouhumes arriving. Their health started to get better and they got to know their surroundings better. Some days the park would have more humans than other days but they worked out when would be the best times to leave the warren.

The main competitors for the food left by the humans were the birds. The rats and mice were also getting food but the Mouhumes often would chase them away or kill them if they were in small numbers.

They made devices that would kill the rats as they were bigger than Mouhumes. Those left at the warren had little fighting skills; the main fighters had left along with Ratty and Tube. These Mouhumes had to depend on outwitting everything in their way. They learned fast, they had to for their own survival.

Weeks had passed since Rug and others had moved away. If only they had stayed, they could have had more than enough food. The community was now growing fast and they were all healthy young

Mouhumes. Not one Mouhume was what you would call a leader but they worked as a group. Each one was known for his or hers own abilities.

What had been a small proportion of the Mouhume community was now split into three groups. What ever became of any other group was unknown to them. Those who had gone with Tube would not know about the split at the warren, so as far as they knew they would still be there.

Those who had gone with Rug would not know about how well they were doing now. They had split up into different parts of the area; to them it might have been different worlds. The only similar thing was humans had a part in their survival.

Now unknown to them they were starting to depend on humans, much more than they should or would have if they had noticed.

Some days were quiet but two days a week, one particular, was always full of humans especially if it was a sunny day. The grass area was full of humans sitting, eating and running around. Some Mouhumes would hide in the long grass or on the embankment watching.

Some humans would be kicking and chasing a round thing.
The Mouhumes could not understand why they would kick something then run after it. Then more humans would join in doing the same thing. It was very strange.

They would then sit down, eat their food dropping little bits or even laughing as they threw it at each other. Not all humans did this. Some would put it in the large circular containers. The Mouhumes found those hard to get into but they had worked out a way of getting into them and retrieving food.

As always birds would be their main competitors as they did not show any concern about the humans being there. The Mouhumes did not want anyone seeing them so they had to wait until it was safe to collect the food.

They had dug deeper into the soft sand to store what food they could. It was cooler the deeper they went. So this worked out well for them, the food would last longer. They had worked out that during bad weather humans did not go to the park so food was harder to find. There were fewer berries growing here, nothing like the amount growing where they used to live.

Other wild animals were mostly in packs so it was sometimes dangerous to hunt them. But then it was a risk if they had eaten the poisonous food sometimes put out by the human who lived in the bungalow in the car park.

That was a great risk, more than they had ever known before. Not just finding the food but the danger of eating contaminated food. Contaminated food was infecting whatever was eating it then it was being passed onto whatever was eating that. They still had to take the risk sometimes but not as much as they might have had to do if the park had not been so busy.

They soon discovered or recognised the odour of the food that had been poisoned and that of what had eaten it. The aroma had often been on the breath of an enemy so they would avoid killing that animal for food.

Some food was found in parts of the woodland: wood nuts, elderberries and even some raspberries growing wild but it was not enough to sustain a growing community of Mouhumes. Some of the food supply could be preserved, but some had to be eaten straightaway.

Everything had grown now. When they arrived it was near the end of winter so food was on low supply but now this was summer and things were starting to grow. It was a good spot to stay at this time.

They learned to keep food supplies in the deepest part of the burrow, not just for the coolness but also to keep the smell away from other predators who might stumble upon their food.

No other creature they knew kept food for a later date. When winter came other creature numbers decreased due to the lack of food. Some became aggressive and would raid almost anything due to desperation. The Mouhumes knew this. It was something they had always known, even at their last home, so they had precautions in place.

Something new to them was the river and what was in and around the river. Such as fish, frogs and other reptile's even newts lived near the river. They often caught a newt or a frog. The first time they tried to eat a frog they all stuck out their tongues trying to rub the taste off on something. But most would often be sick.

Frogs had a taste on the skin to help protect them and the Mouhumes did not like this at all. Once they had tried them out of desperation they knew not to try them again. The newts, on the other hand, they liked but they were too fast for them to catch, until they found ways to catch them.

The fish were something else they had never had before and there were allsorts in the river. Some were far too big for them to catch. Just like eels. They had seen the eels take hold of a rat and swallow. Some were only small but they were very aggressive so they kept away from them as well.

These were all new things that they would have to learn to understand or try to work around or even kill them. Whatever way, they would have to make the most of it. They were now content and with numbers growing, they had little ones to feed and take care of.

Chapter 10
Mousey

AT LEAST TWO days had passed since Ruddy had been seen. Tube and Ratty were concerned and it was now beginning to show. This was not like Ruddy to disappear. She might go and do her own thing but she would always be back or at the least leave some sort of clue. All they knew was that she had left the garden, she had gone to where the fairies were and she had not returned, had the fairies killed her?

Mousey was standing with Ratty. Ratty was now on the war path and his temper was short. Mousey knew this so he had to be careful with anything he said and how he said it after all he was the one who had persuaded Tube and Ratty that he should talk to Ruddy and help her.

In Ratty's mind, it was Mousey who was to blame and only him. He told Mousey it was up him to find Ruddy before this day was over. Mousey told Ratty that he had no idea where to start looking because he had already looked. But Ratty was having none of this. Mousey could find out anything Ratty replied with sarcasm and anger in his voice, he then gave Mousey a look that turned him cold with fear.

Mousey knew what he had to do. This time it would be different, not like what he had done just days before, a quick look! This time it had to be done properly. So Mousey left the shed then he went into the next door's garden.

Where had he lost sight of Ruddy and why had she not left him any signs? Once again Mousey went into the house that had the deep hole. There was nothing there just plants, some tall and some not so tall. Mousey climbed up on to one of the tallest plant so that he could observe what was around from a higher view. Nothing seemed to be out of place.

He looked to see if he could find any fairies: there were none that he could see so he called out for them. There was a little panic in his voice as he had no idea what to expect. Still nothing! Had these fairies harmed Ruddy? Were they in hiding ready to pick off any straying Mouhume? Mousey thought to himself, after all they could hide better than Mouhumes. It was as if they just appeared from out of nowhere.

Fear started to take over his thoughts. He was alone in a place where the fairies had made their home. What could he do? He had called for them to come out and face him. What if they did? He knew that he would not be able to hide and the fact that he was scared meant that he was not thinking right!

He started to think that this was a bad idea and started to go back down the plant with the idea of going back altogether. Then the thought of Ratty and the look he gave him just before he left. He gave a little sigh. He was doomed in every way. Half way down the plant he stopped suddenly, his head was almost ready to explode with all the thoughts going through it.

He knew he would have to go back with an answer of some sort. More importantly maybe evidence of one kind or another. He called again for the fairy that saved Ruddy. He did not know its' name or even if that one would come but he thought if he shouted fairy it would get some sort of attention.

Still nothing, he finally got back to the ground and stood thinking. He decided he should use his senses and his awareness. He stood with his eyes shut and let his mind become one with what was around him: he could hear the birds not just because they were singing but the sound of their wings flapping; insects were landing near him; and the slight breeze blowing leaves on the plants. He could sense all of this and more, so why could he not sense the fairies?

He started to look around the garden. It had a number of model houses. They were all different in shape and style. He went into each one some had rooms and other ones were covering a hole. In the hole there was nothing, no passageways, nothing, why?

He started to doubt his own skill and that was where he always found answers. He searched almost every inch of that garden, except near the human house. He went as near as he dare but in his heart he knew Ruddy would never get that close to a human home.

Time was getting on. He was feeling a little hungry and he had not brought anything with him. He did not dare go back without something to tell the elders so he started to look for something to eat in the next garden.

Halfway up in the garden he made his way through the garden hedge. He knew there was a possibility of food lying on the ground. He was right. The birds had brought it but not eaten it yet but he would have to be quick. He ran across the lawn and took a handful of old broken biscuits.

He never stopped running until he was on the other side of the garden under a large area covered with shrubbery. He started to eat his food: the biscuits had currents, raisins and other fruit mixed in. It was ideal to give him some energy. As Mousey sat looking around for potential danger he saw the human from the garden where they had made their home. He was looking around the pond area. Mousey wondered what could he be looking for?

Mousey decided to go somewhere better for a look. The birds were still eating the remaining food on the grass. He stuffed what he had left into his fur jacket so that he could have it later. Once again he hid among the plants in between the hedge. It was a good spot to hide and see what the human was up to.

The human had a long stick. He was poking it into the plants around the pond and then he came down the garden a little way. He seemed to be looking for something. What was it? Mousey knew he would have to find out. His curiosity was taking hold of him.

Then from the corner of his eye he saw Ratty hiding on the other side of the garden looking at him. Then suddenly Mousey remembered his task was to find Ruddy. His brain was now in overdrive. What if the human could lead him to Ruddy?

Suddenly there was a tap on his shoulder. He almost jumped out of the shrubbery onto the lawn but a hand held him back, it pulled him to the ground with a thud quickly putting a hand over his mouth to keep him quiet.

It was Ratty. As Mousey had been daydreaming about what he should and should not do Ratty had came around the edge of the garden in between the bushes. Ratty when he had spotted Mousey had seen this look on his face before and knew that he needed waking up.

The human had not noticed this happening and was still looking around he stood for a little longer then went back into his house.

The birds had not been disturbed; they just carried on eating the last little bits of food. Ratty looked down at Mousey as he got up, he then asked him if he had forgotten what he was meant to be doing? Mousey did not say a word he just shook his head.

Ratty gave Mousey a hard slap around his head knocking him back onto the ground. Mousey stayed there for a moment until Ratty had gone away. Now he had understood the desperation in everyone's mind to find Ruddy. Off he went back to where he had left off. In his mind he was going to find Ruddy one way or another.

He went back near the plant he had climbed up earlier. Near the top he had to stop to have a bit of his food again and a little drink from the flower that had been holding a little rainwater. Now he was ready to do what he was known best for, better than any other Mouhume ... and that was finding things out.

He was more determined now and focused on the job in hand. He had already called for the fairy and not had any response so they must be behind the disappearance of Ruddy.

His razor-sharp thorn from a bush nearby was going to get the evidence as to what and where Ruddy might be. He had not seen everything that had happened to Ruddy when she had been thrown down from the sky but he had seen her on the ground and what other Mouhumes had said about what they had seen.

So he was going to strike first, wound it, then ask questions later. He went in the direction he had last seen Ruddy go. It was towards a big dense hedge. He stopped. Why would she head towards that? Not even a tiny mouse would be able to go through that without difficulty?

But he was determined to find out. It had to be way into it and he was going to find out. As he got near the hedge the difference in the daylight made him stop so that his eyes could adjust. Something was not right as he stood near the hedge. He looked at it but his eyes were still not adjusting, he could not focus properly.

He took a few steps back. Stood a while then he heard a noise from up the garden. It was the old man who lived in this house. He was calling for something or someone; the old man had a tray with something on it that he thought looked like food.

Mousey stepped back and back again watching the human all the time. The human was still up the garden, at a table and placing whatever was on the tray onto the table. He carried on watching as he took another step backwards, but before he knew it he was in the hedge that had made his eyes blurry. He went backwards into it. The strange thing was, it was as if he could see through it and it was around him but not touching him? He could move around and nothing was stopping him. It was as if the branches from the hedge were there but not, there appeared to be no restriction.

At this time he had took his eyes off what was going on up the garden. He was too engrossed with his new surroundings. This was magic. Had he discovered some magical power that he could go through and into plants without any restriction?

He stood for longer than he should have in his new surroundings, making only slight movements with hands. This was great he thought. Nothing was stopping him, he could move through solid objects.

The aroma was not of anything he had come across before. It was not something he wanted to be around any longer than he needed to be. Mousey looked up the garden once again. The human was still up there. But to his surprise he could see a number of fairies: one on the shoulder of the human and others eating from the table the human had put the food on.

But the human was still there. Suddenly he was flying in the air, two fairies had him a shoulder each heading towards the human. He had no time to do anything before he was dropped onto the table where some of the fairies were eating.

Those who were eating turned around sharply almost snarling at Mousey and ready to attack him. The human picked Mousey up by the scruff of the neck.
Mousey being dressed in a fur skin from a mouse looked like a mouse at first glance.

Looking straight into the human's eye Mousey could see what was going to happen next. The expression on the human's face told him that he was going to kill him.

Mousey never took his eyes off him. Then the human pulled back his arm ready to throw Mousey as far as he could. Mousey felt sick in his stomach. It was like nothing he had ever experienced before. He was hoping to pass out but no, in no time at all he was flying in the air spinning around with no idea in which direction he was going. The whole world, sky and ground was twirling and twisting into one but still he never passed out. He was expecting a thud, unbearable pain and then everything to go black.

Chapter 11
Woodlands

BACK IN THE woods Rug and others made camp. They had found some trees with passageways under the roots so they did not have a lot to do, just a little modifying here and there. They decided this would be the best place for now. It was not that far away from the humans so they could go and raid the gardens for food when they were struggling with the resources in the woodland. There was plenty of wildlife which meant they could feed on plenty. There were new plants they could make use of.

Rug always said that once they had set up somewhere to live he would go back and get those left in the park area. He knew he would have to go back sooner rather than later to help them as they had little food. He would have to take food supplies with him but first he would have to make sure they had enough in his new camp.

This would take a day or two as they had to find out what was around them and how they would take advantage of the new area. They knew food was put out for the birds at certain times in the day. The only downside was that the birds could be aggressive and sometimes the humans would stand at a distance to watch the birds feeding. Some humans put the food out and walked away. That was the time not to hesitate and go for it. The idea was to run and grab as much as possible and get back to safety.

This area was not all that different to where they had once lived; the only difference was being so close to the humans. They would adapt soon and make the best out of the situation.

The passageways they had from one tree to another were already there, so this saved them a lot of work. They only needed to dig out chambers for their own space. The sandy ground under the trees had clay in parts but they could find use for it and make things they would need from the clay.

It did not take them long to make their new home. It was as safe as they could make it using knowledge they had gained though the different experiences they had encountered in their lives. Safety and defensive areas were made to keep them safe if they were ever attacked underground.

The main concern was all of those dead rats. Had the rest of them moved on or were they still in the area? Rats were strong and fearless fighters and came in large numbers which made them almost impossible to defeat. Even though a large number were dead and it would have made a big hole in the numbers, rats multiplied quickly so their numbers would increase in no time.

One thing the Mouhumes had though was intelligence and skills that might help outwit any enemies that were large in numbers. They had encountered rats a number of times. Rats ran all over the place scurrying and killing almost everything in front of them. They were a big enemy to all creatures.

Rug had been told this from a young age and from what he had seen nothing was going to change his mind. They plagued the land, leaving behind them death and famine. They would eat everything in their path then move on and then another pack would follow.

The food that had been poisoned would put off any other Rats from coming but no doubt they would be back at some stage. The others must have moved on but Rug knew they needed defence weapons in and around the area they lived in.

Rug was now a leader and not a bad one at all but he still wanted to find Tube, Ratty and the others. He would not rest until he found some sort of trail. He still had no idea where they would be or even if they were still alive. Rug knew they had a strong chance as Tube had taken some of the strongest warriors.

Rug knew he had some young up and coming fearless fighters but they still lacked the experience of those who had left. This was his main fear. He now knew he had made a mistake, his own lack of knowledge had been his error for demanding Ruddy to go. He had no idea that she had a lot of followers, more than he had ever thought. He believed they would all be too frightened to leave with her and that he would be the new conqueror.

Now he was frightened. He told those who had come with him that he would be the leader and take them to safety but now doing it was far harder than he had ever thought it would be. They depended on him and already he had left those who were too weak in the park.

He started to doubt his own ability but those around him seemed more than happy to go along with most of his decisions. This gave him some comfort. He would still be in charge for now but when he thought of Tube he began to think how happy he would be if he could pass the leadership back to him without question.

His group soon developed their own habits they all had there own roles. Some would be out during the day gathering food; others would be out during the early hours of the morning, still in darkness, collecting food and setting traps, The Mouhumes knew they would put defences and traps up that would slow down if not kill a potential enemy and all those in their camp knew what to do, when and how to do it.

They had it as secure as they possibly could. Not a lot could come and attack them without been hurt or killed and to help prevent attacks from large numbers they made a lot of harmful hidden traps with lots of sharp bits sticking up. The traps were set all around the camp, thorns were placed under the fallen leaves, sharp end pointing up so if a dog was to wander near their home it would get a thorn in its pad and head back to where it came from. They also had traps to kill smaller animals such as rats, mice, moles and rabbits. They might be smaller than most things but they were just as dangerous.

It would take at least six of them with experience to kill a rabbit. Then there were squirrels, they were as fast as any Mouhume but three times bigger. The Mouhumes were no match for them. They could move around trees and the ground at ease with speed and suppleness. As for rabbits they were pretty much grounded so a Mouhume could get extra height by going up a tree or a bush if and when they needed to.

They picked an area with trees that had good long strong roots so they could have a warren between a number of trees with plenty of space and places they could go and hide if the need arose.

The next thing Rug had to do, was to return to the park area and bring those he left behind back to their new home just as he promised;

Chapter 12
Tube's Action

TUBE WAS TALKING to some of the Mouhumes when he was interrupted. Scallop had run in all flustered. He ran straight to Tube who was taken by surprise but had reacted quickly and he took Scallop's feet away straight from underneath him... Scallop fell to the floor.

Scallop quickly jumped to his feet, two Mouhumes got hold of him restraining him. Tube quietly asked what the matter was. Why was he out of control? This was not like Scallop. This was not how Scallop behaved!

Scallop broke free from the hold of the two Mouhumes and got a firm hold of Tube's arm and whispered something in his ear. The colour from Tube's face drained almost grey. His legs weakened slightly but Scallop held on to him.

Tube knew he had to show strength in front of the others. He demanded that everyone leave and sent for Ratty to come straight away as it was a matter of great urgency. Everyone left as they were told, leaving Scallop and Tube alone.

Tube told Scallop they would discuss what he had just been told but he had to wait for Ratty. Not another word could be spoken until Ratty arrived.

Once Ratty arrived Scallop started telling them from start to finish. Starting from when he had seen Mousey in the garden next door doing his detective work.
His story was something unbelievable it was hard to understand what they were now being told; it was something they could hardly get their heads around as he explained it.

He told them that he had stayed hidden and out of sight. As he was always amazed at how Mousey could find out things so he thought he would keep an eye on him to learn how he did it so well.

He explained that Mousey was going into the small houses: in and out looking around them and going from one area to another. He was also going up tall plants then down and then up another.

Then the human from the house next door came out. He was making some sort of sound and putting food on the table. Scallop had thought the food was for the birds but to his surprise the fairies came from out of nowhere.

Scallop carried on with his story. Tube and Ratty did not say a word. The fairies had been on plants or hidden around the plants? It was hard to say but they just appeared.

Mousey had seemed to disappear as much as Scallop could see from his hiding place. He looked around he could not see Mousey but there were one or two plants and objects in his way so he could not get a clear view at all.

However he did see one of the fairies who had picked up Ruddy. He recognised her by her torn wings. She was clearly a fairy who had been in more than her fair share of conflicts. Her battle scars were clear to see.

She had a stern look about her. She once would have been beautiful but instead she was full of scars, she looked disappointed, stressed and worried.

Scallop said that she reminded him of Ruddy but had a different pursuit. That much became clear in the strange circumstances. The story began to unfold.

"Mousey was unseen then suddenly, like Ruddy, he was pulled out from somewhere. Two fairies had him and dropped him on the table where the others were feeding around the human. The fairy with the damaged wings was on the table when Mousey was dropped."

"She must have gotten a fright. She turned quickly and was ready to attack but the human picked Mousey up and pulled his arm back to stop them from hurting him. There was some movement but then they settled down."

"That's when I saw that Mousey must have passed out. His body was lame and floppy. The human put him on the table. Some of the fairies crowded around. I could not see what happened next. The human walked away and Mousey was gone."

"The next thing was that young fairy at my side. I thought that I was going to be the next one. One by one they were picking us off. So I pulled my thorn out and was ready to attack when that fairy with the damage wings came. She told me to calm down but in a way that I knew was … right and true."

"She asked me to follow her up the garden which I did. The human had gone into the house but I was still unsure what was going to happen. I still held on to my thorn ready to kill or be killed. She led me into the outhouse."

Tube and Ratty sat listening with amazement. All would become clear as they sat without interruption.

"As I went into the outhouse it was Mousey that I saw first. He was still unconscious. They said that he would be alright. It was the shock of being picked up by the human. Ted that's what he's called, Ted. Anyway he passed out. Ted had put him in the outhouse away from any harm,"

"That's when I saw Ruddy lying in a box with some sort of bedding. She was nursing a baby. She had been carrying a baby. She had been pregnant. That's why she had not been herself these last few days. The fall had brought it on faster than it should have."

The gasp Tube and Ratty made was of relief. She was ok. Well as ok as a mother could be. She was now with the fairies and they were looking after her until she felt able to come back.

Scallop carried on with what he had seen and what he'd been told. The fairy that was going to attack Mousey was also the mother of Capheus. Once again Ratty and Tube looked on with confused expressions.

Scallop told them as if they should have known who Capheus was; Capheus was the one who Ruddy had thrown on the ground. It was his mother. Just like Ruddy she was a fighter. He said that with superiority.

Ratty asked Scallop what it was about this particular fairy? Why was he so taken with her? It was clear to Ratty and Tube, his head was turned. Rightly or wrongly it was too soon to tell so they let him tell rest of his story.

As they had found out the days before, the fairies could talk and understand most living creatures and they get along with just about everything.

Scallop wanted to tell them everything that he had seen and been told. It was something he could hardly understand, so telling Tube and Ratty with their knowledge of most things they might be able to help him to understand. After all, it might not be all that wonderful.

Some of the fairies had two wings and some had four wings. Some had so many colours they looked like flowers. Some were big and some were tiny.

There were not many older males, just young males. You could tell that some female fairies were a lot older and yet it seemed they done most things such as defending, hunting for food and talking to the human.

As he told Tube and Ratty about what he knew it seemed that the fairy world had a lot going for it. Tube asked about Mousey, when would he be back to give his account?

Scallop told them that someone would have to go to see them as he was still shaky. They did not want him to get hurt by any predators such as birds, cats and any other danger that might be around.

Now they had to decide who and when they would go to collect Mousey and see what help they could be to Ruddy.

Tube was thinking why had they not told anyone about Ruddy? They would have seen us. He sat for a while going over a few things in his head and looking at it in different ways but still could not justify why they had not made contact.

Tube sent Scallop away so he could talk with Ratty. He told Ratty his thoughts. Ratty also had similar thoughts. Was it a trap? It was a hard thing to decide but Tube said that he would go and collect Mousey and more importantly, see how Ruddy was.

Tube had a way of working out what actions they might take from the way they held their bodies, just little signals. It was something in the eyes that made him react without hesitation.

He might not be as young as most but he had more experience than any. He would go with only Scallop. That way they would see that they went in peace. Ratty stayed back but gathered all those he could, without making it obvious to any hidden eyes.

Scallop took Tube straight to the outhouse where Ruddy and Mousey were. Two fairies' came, none of whom Scallop had seen earlier. These two were smaller and both were bright in colour: red, green and yellow. Both were beautiful. They could hardly stay in the same place for more than a second or two.

Tube could not get anything from this action. It was not aggression or anything else, more than their behaviour. Tube thought because of their size, being less than half of a Mouhume, they might be fearful of being swooped up from a bird. After all they were a lot smaller than some of the fairies they had already seen.

This was all new for the Mouhumes. They had never had anything to do with other creatures, apart from fighting or killing. Now they seemed to be receiving help, help they never asked for or had ever been given before. So why were the fairies so keen to give them help? This was going to be something Tube would have to find out. He had a suspicious mind and rightfully so.

He was led into the washhouse. Scallop stayed at the doorway. Tube was led up on to one of the benches. Ruddy was in a shoebox with a hole cut out. As soon as she heard Tube she was out the box with her little baby in her arms. Her face was full of smiles and pride.

Tube walked to her. This must have been the first time he let his emotions be seen. A smile from ear to ear and a tear ran down his face. Ruddy put her arm around him and cuddled him. There were countless things he wanted to ask her but this was not the time.

Mousey emerged from behind another box, full of smiles that were short lived. Tube gave him a glance and Mousey knew that he had let him down. Now was not the time, this moment was for Ruddy.

Was she ready to go back to camp? Was she in good health? Was she getting everything she needed? Tube fired question after question at her. Ruddy smiled as she did not get time to reply to the first question when another was asked.

Then to the side of Ruddy appeared a fairy. It was the one who had saved Ruddy. His wings were still a bit tattered from the fall but otherwise he was ok and still full of high spirits. Then his mother came. She was as big as Tube in height. Her wings were torn from previous fights. Scallop was right, she had a beautiful face but one of worry. Tube looked at her looking at her son. It was the worry on her face, a parent's worry for a child who was now almost fully grown.

The adventures he would now want to do not knowing all the danger out there, but still wanting to find out all new things and learn like his parents had too.

His mother wanted to hold onto him as long as she could. A male fairy could only mate once and then the male died. So having a male was a mother's heartache. A male would be protected by all the adults but being a male he would find mischief and that's why he needed watching.

He had been watching Ruddy for a number of days but got too close to her and that was why she attacked him. He might have been hard to see but her instinct told her something was near. He thought with his hard-to-see camouflage. He would be ok getting near other living things even though he never thought they could see him.

His mother started to talk to Tube. She told him her name and her son's name. She was called Glow and he was called Capheus. She explained why he was protected so much. There were two other males of similar age and they would be moving to other fairy communities in the near future. The males from other communities would move to theirs and so on. That would be the last time they would see their son. It was both a joyful and sad time. This would happen only once a year.

They stood chatting for a while. Tube was keen to know as much about these wonderful creatures. He would learn so much from them but now was the time to go back to his own with Ruddy, the baby, Mousey and Scallop.

As they left the outhouse a number of fairies came and said their goodbyes. It was only the next garden but they said they would not interfere in that garden anymore so the Mouhumes could have their own space.

Tube was told a little about those who lived in the house. Jack was the man who sat in the early hours looking out the window and the woman who comes and goes they did not know her name. It was Jack who spent most his time in the garden but not so much recently, he was walking badly so he just sat looking out the window.

The fairies had never shown themselves to anyone else but Ted. They could talk to most living things but humans could not understand them. They could understand humans. They needed to know a lot more.

Tube went back and the welcome Ruddy got was amazing. The legend was back and had a baby. Word spread quickly around the camp so all day she had visitors wishing her well. In the meantime Ratty and Tube had to talk to Mousey about his experience. This would be a long and detailed discussion, one that Mousey was not looking forward to.

Chapter 13
Return to the Park

RUG AND FOUR others headed back to the park. It was early evening but they still had the cover of the trees. Rug had thought if they left now by the time they had to cross over the roads it would be quiet and there was less likelihood of them being seen from any harmful eyes. As it worked out he was right. They scurried in and out of shrubbery, not coming across many dangers. They were fast and now they were near the top of the hill above the park.

The nightlight was dull but it was still light enough to see the bottom of the hill. Cars were still in the car park and noises were coming from the grass area. Humans were still running around.

Rug pointed out the area that he wanted to go to. They all nodded but now it was time to take a break. They had travelled a great distance without stopping. Rug had picked the fastest and strongest for this journey. They were fearless and proved themselves many times before.

After they stopped and had a short rest they decided it was now time to go forward with the last part of the journey. They would need all the energy they had as with the humans still around, they would have to move with speed and agility.

Running alongside the green area, there were trees and blackberry bushes that were good for them as they knew they would have cover, especially from an overhead threat. As soon as they got to the end of the bushes they stopped to assess what they would do next. The humans were now thinning out but some were still near the area they wanted to be.

Rug wanted to be back at his new burrow before morning but at the same time he did not want to be seen by humans. And at this moment he could not make out how many humans were still there. He could see six but there were also noises coming from places out of his sight. They sounded close to the area where they were heading. After a short consideration of what to do or not to do they made a run for it. They criss-crossed each other in and out of the clearing and into some sheltered areas. They may have been spread out but they were still in sight of each other.

With only a few yards to go, they would be in one of the burrows entrance. Rug was, at this point, a bit worried. He was wondering if they would still be there, or more importantly, still alive. He had left food for them but some had been so poorly, he knew that it would take more than what he had left behind.

It was getting dark outside; the warren would be in total darkness. There would be no light at all deep inside. Mouhume eyes took a little time to adjust to different lights like darkness but once they did they could see reasonably well. The danger was that if they ran straight into the burrow they would not see anything for a short time, so they could be in an unsafe, even fragile state for a moment. Rug was sure that those who were with him would be ready for any attack.

The humans were now in the distance. He gave the signal and they ran into the burrow stopping a little way in so that their eyes could adjust. They pulled out their weapons all made from thorns and bones from small animals they had killed for food.

As they went deeper into the burrow they could hear sounds coming from below. The sound was muffled from the sandy walls. They headed down with caution. They were unsure what it was. Then they could smell something. It was a strange odour, not one that Rug had come across before. It was not unpleasant but nothing that he knew.

Rug suddenly stopped. One of the Mouhumes behind him almost went into his back. They were at the end of that tunnel. The sound was just around the corner. Rug listened to see if he could work out what it was.

There was still a lot of noise and still muffled. He thought he would just go for it and round the corner which he did. The other four went with him. The sound of a twig snapping; a cry for help, then the sound of thudding, bodies being hit then it was over. Silence nothing was moving.

Then there was the sound of bodies dropping to the ground with a thud and then laughter and shrieks of surprise.

The Mouhumes left in the old rabbit warren had made a net from roots and hid it under the sandy ground so when they had a surprise visit it would tangle up who or what ever had stepped onto it. With two

Mouhumes pulling up the ends it gave them time to attack those in the net.

It was only sheer luck they were not run through with a thorn on the end of a long shaft. Something they had not finished yet so they had to bash the enemy with clubs first then with anything sharp they had, at least until the trap was ready. This had saved them.

Rug and the others were let loose with hugs and laughter from those in the warren. A lot was needed to be said from both sides and it would be, but it had not turned out how Rug had thought it would. Rug had thought this was going to be a rescue mission, there and back taking home those who were still alive, if any.

Rug knew the warren as well as those who now had made it their home. They went to the biggest part so they could talk. Rug was told after he had left, there were a number of those who were so ill that they had died because of the time of year, poor weather and the food supplies were almost none.

Then when the weather started to get better and humans came with picnics. They began dropping food and putting food in bins. It was collected as soon as they could get it. Now they had a good storage and had more than enough food. Not all the food was from humans, some came from plants that were growing around the woodland area.

Rug was taken to the storage area. He was astonished at how much they had and how well they all looked. There were young Mouhumes on the way. It had become a strong group and they seemed to have worked out what they needed to survive. It was done so quickly too.

Rug told them about his journey and his new home. He was asked about Tube and Ratty and the others. He sank his head, told them that he could not find them and that there was no sign of them.

He was reminded about the way they left and how they would not want to leave a trail. He agreed time was getting on. Then he was asked if he would like to stay for the night. He sat for a while and agreed that it would be for the best. This gave him an opportunity to see how they managed and get to know their way of doing things whilst being so close to the humans.

He could not help himself but he had to find out what the smell was. They showed him it was cooked meat that kept longer than other food stuff. It came from the top of the hill. They had no name for it but the other food stuff came from the same place.

They told him how humans eat it a lot but throw a lot away too. He was then told more Mouhumes came back into the burrow with more food from humans. Things like part eaten sandwiches, kebabs, chips, broken biscuits, crisps and just about anything a human would take on a picnic. Some of the Mouhumes made the empty crisp packets into clothing to help them keep dry when it was raining.

Rug was surprised how well they had come on. He wanted to know about the trap that he was held up in, how it worked and so on …

He stayed the night and early hours of the morning. He was to go back home with a small party from the warren so that if they needed to know where his camp was they could come. That way they could keep in touch and help out each other when needing extra help with food or anything.

As they headed home to the woodland the Mouhumes had already been as far as the chip shop but not much further. Now they were in new land and going in and out of gardens then finally into the woodland area were Rug had his camp.

There were more trees than at the park so they had more cover. The Mouhumes from the park made little symbols so they could find their way back. They also saw some that were already made from Rug when he first explored that area.

In the park the Mouhumes asked if there were any signs from Tube and the others when they left, he told them none that they could see.

Daylight was now upon them so the park Mouhumes would have to stay until later that night. This would give them time to discover the area. They had brought food supplies with them, more than they would need. They gave Rug's camp some to try. The kebab meat took a bit of getting used to. It was edible but only as a last resort.

The parkland Mouhumes were shown around the area. None of them knew how near they were to Tube's camp. In truth they were only across the road and five gardens down. If they knew they might have found each other.

    This was going to be Rug's next thing to do: he had to find Tube and the others, to help them if needed. He was not going to stop until he found them.

Chapter 14
Awkward Reunion

RUG HAD MADE his mind up. He was going to spend the next few days looking for Tube and the others. He was a little more experienced now. Rug had realised that he was wrong for trying to take over the leadership and also for making demands about Ruddy.

He had convinced himself that she had brought danger to the rabbit warren but now he knew that it was not as he had thought, before they had known the dangers around them. Now the danger was all new, not just from predators but the real danger came from having very little food.

He had to find them, he just had to. No-one in his tree stump had any idea how to store food. He realized this when he went back to the park warren. They had worked it out: they knew what food and the best way to do it and it worked well.

He had done the right thing going back to the warren. From the short time he was there he learnt all about how to store food and also how to make netting from thin roots to trap enemies. He knew there was so much more that he needed to learn.

He had already looked around the area on a number occasions so what they would now have to do was one of two things: they could go higher up into the woods or go over the road to the other side and look around the houses there. This was not something Rug wanted to do but, he had considered it a number of times. Still a little unsure as he always thought that Tube would never go near humans unless, something made them cross paths.

Rug and some of his camp had already been as far up into the woodland area as they dared so this meant there was only one option left and that was to go over the road to see what was there. At least they would know and then they could get on with looking somewhere else if they didn't find them.

Rug with his companions went into the nearest garden. It was early in the morning; there were no lights on in the houses. They crept along the side of the house into the front garden, stopping just outside the hedge.

They looked up and down the road to see if anyone or anything might be there. The streets looked empty. Higher up the road a house light had just been turned on so Rug knew the humans were starting to wake up. It was now or never to cross the road.

They took no time crossing the road: slightly splitting up due to the fact that straight over the road was a garden with a wall around it. So now they had to go to the back of the house with a garden between them.

It might have only been a garden between them but there was a big difference between the two gardens. The Mouhumes who had gone to the higher garden had to fathom out how to get around the back of the house to meet the others.

The house had been empty. Most of the contents such as the old carpets and broken cupboards were blocking the walkway at the side of the house. The rubbish was attracting vermin: rats and mice. This was not something two Mouhumes wanted to come across by themselves. The smell coming from the carpet was terrible.

They had to decide and decide quickly if they wanted to go that way. It would be the quickest but not the healthiest for more than one reason. Whatever they were going to do would have to be quick as more and more lights were being turned on in the houses. From previous experience this could only mean one thing, animals: dogs and cats would be coming out the houses. No doubt some of that smell belonging to dogs.

They looked at each other with disappointment on their faces. They knew that Rug would be at the back end of the house now and waiting for them. They would just have to go over it. It was almost as high as the door. It had just been thrown out the house in a heap.

Rug was at the back of the other house in the garden looking for the two Mouhumes. He knew they should have been there by now, so he decided to go and look for them as he went into the next door's garden he was still expecting them to appear at anytime. As Rug walked around the corner his eyes could not believe what he was looking at. It was a mountain of rubbish and even from where he was standing the stench was overbearing. He had to grin; the two who had gone that way were now falling from the heap then running as fast as they could from it, stopping just in front of Rug.

The rotten carpets together with the smell of old food, cigarette smoke and also dog and cat scent, was more than they could put up with. They had never come across anything like this before.

Rug tried to keep his distance from the two Mouhumes but they kept getting near him as they tried telling him what it was like. It got to the stage where Rug had to tell them to go back to camp and get cleaned up which they agreed without question. The smell was turning their stomachs. As quick as they arrived they returned to camp only this time they left the way Rug had arrived they were not going over that heap again.

The only thing was, this left Rug with only one Mouhume for help. Still he was not going back. What danger could there be? He thought all the gardens are similar, a dog here, a cat there and humans coming into the gardens putting food out. It was nothing he had not seen before; it was just like that on the other side of the street.

He would just have to be careful and as there were only two of them there would be less possibility of them being seen. So eventually they went down to the hedge weaving in and out until they reached the bottom of the hedge.

At the end of the garden there was a large grassed area open to any amount of danger. It was no good for a Mouhume to attempt venturing across it so there was only one thing to do and that was to go as he had intended out of sight.

As they travelled down another four gardens they could hear water running. It was not that far away, maybe two or so gardens away. The noise of humans going out to work made them find cover for a while. They might have lived in the woods but they had come across the same thing at certain times of the day. All they could do was hide and hope that nothing would come along to hurt them. All they could do was to rest, have a snack and a drink from their pouch. Time went by slowly. Humans were going to work and young humans were going to school then finally things went quiet.

At least on the other side of the road this did not last as long. The humans seemed to be heading towards this side of the road for some reason.

Now Rug could now move on. Rug and his companion decided to head towards the water to fill up their water pouches and collect any food they might find. They were only two gardens away from the sound of water when they came across a garden with a gate. The gate was leading on to the big lawn area. This was not strange in itself but what was happening was!

Rug and the Mouhume with him stood back in astonishment. They had never seen anything like it. The Mouhume with Rug rubbed his eyes not once but twice. He also pinched Rug's arm to see if he was awake. Rug turned and slapped him over the head. Yes he was awake and yes what he was seeing right in front his eyes was happening.

Rug was, in a way, pleased the young Mouhume nipped his arm because he was also wondering if he was dreaming. Now he had to make a decision, what could he do? Was he to go and show himself or was he to stand back to see what was going to happen next. His thoughts were all over the place. He was just about to step out when his arm was pulled back.

The young Mouhume pulled him back and whispered they should stay and observe for a while. Rug knew this was right but did not like hearing it from a younger Mouhume. Still he nodded.

As they watched it became even more astonishing. Things they had never seen or heard of were happening right in front of them. They stayed hidden in the bushes and long grass that was growing at the base of the prickly bush. Rug wanted to know more about what they were watching but they would stay hidden, just for now.

As they watched, a Mouhume called Woozy was pulling the gate open he was also getting help from a creature Rug had never seen before. They seemed to be working hand in hand. The Mouhume was on the ground pulling the rope and the other creature was pulling the catch open.

It was an old gate that was held on to a brick wall, one of the rusted hinges just holding on. It looked like it was ready to be pulled off once and for all. Rug wondered if that was what they were trying to do, pull the rotten gate away from the post. But why would they do that?

He could see no reason. If the gate was open, the garden would be open to any predator. Then before his eyes a dog came running straight towards Woozy. Rug pulled his sharp thorn out, ready to go and attack the dog.

He jumped out from the hedge and headed towards the dog. Then he stopped. The dog with slaver drooling and dribbling from its mouth licked Woozy from toe to head. Not once, but twice covering him with its dribble. Woozy just rubbed its muzzle as if he was its friend.

Rug stood watching then, it was even more remarkable then he imagined. He could see a young Mouhume sitting just behind the dog's ear; he stood there almost frozen to the spot when the dog charged towards him, lifting her front paw up and knocking Rug backwards onto the ground.

Woozy, still wiping the slaver from his face and body, saw what happened. He called for the dog to stop. The fairy nearby was translating so that the dog could understand. By this time she was standing over Rug, her hot breath upon him. Rug, at this time, closed his eyes thinking that he was going to be killed.

The young Mouhume who was on the back of the dog looked down, Woozy ran over and helped Rug to his feet. Without thinking he started to tell Rug the fairy had called the dog off. Then he told Rug the dog was called Tilly and the young Mouhume was Dash, the son of Ruddy.

It was a lot to take in but Rug listened. The other Mouhume came out from hiding. This made Woozy feel a little insecure. Woozy was still wet from Tilly. His rabbit fur jacket looked as if it had been in a pool of water and it weighed him down slightly. A fur jacket wet was not the best for fast movements but he knew that Tilly and Starlight were nearby, if needed.

Starlight landed beside Woozy. She was almost twice the size of any Mouhume and her strength more than ten Mouhumes together. She liked Woozy and he liked her. They often spent days together with Dash and Tilly. The four, over the last week or two, had become almost inseparable. First thing in the morning and last thing at night, only parting when Tilly had to be in and when Starlight needed to re-energize. That would be at least twice a day, depending on what they had been doing.

Making herself invisible took a lot out of her. It took a lot of energy and could drain a fairy a lot. That was something they would only do in extreme circumstances.

Woozy started to tell Rug that they had missed him but also said they did not know that if they went back to the park whether they would end up fighting or killing each other so they thought it best to stay away.

Woozy knew that Rug was stronger and more than capable to beat him so he just had to play it down as he did not know what Rug was after. More importantly, was he here to hurt Dash. After all, it was Ruddy he had not wanted in the commune.

He had to think quickly. If he headed two more gardens down he would be in the fairies community then the next garden down it would be his. What could he do?

He walked away from Rug and Rug's friend towards Tilly. Tilly bent her head down. He asked Dash if he could get off Tilly and run home with Starlight following him but also asked Starlight to make sure that no one was following them.

Starlight agreed she knew what she had to do. Dash just thought that he had to go home but Starlight knew that she would have to get Ruddy and the others. She had not known all that had happened but she knew enough to get Ruddy and anyone else that was willing.

Dash ran home as quick as he could. Starlight went back and forth, keeping an eye on him but also back tracking, making sure they had not been followed. When Dash got to the big shed he ran straight down into the basement.

Starlight had an idea where Ruddy might be at this time. Two of her other friends followed her; they knew by her expression that something was not right. Starlight went straight to the garden were Buster lived. Tilly lived there as well but Starlight often opened the gate for her so her and Dash could go for a run. Buster was happy enough spending his time in the garden with Ruddy and the other Mouhumes who came in the garden.

Ruddy and her friends were trying to find out how the hedgehog got into the garden. It was every Tuesday without fail then Buster would roll it around the garden getting his face and paws covered in quills.

Ruddy had tried to tell Buster, with the help of Glow, to leave it alone but the temptation was too strong. He had to roll it around then the hedgehog would walk away amused with itself.

Starlight landed on top of Buster's head. She knew that Ruddy would not be that far away. Buster froze to the spot with surprise. This had been the first time a fairy had ever landed on him.

Starlight started to call for Ruddy and Glow. Glow came out from part of the hedging with Ruddy right beside her. Starlight told them what was wrong and also told Ruddy that she had sent Dash home to safety.

Before Ruddy could do or say anything Starlight and Glow had picked her up and were taking her to where Woozy was. This would be the quickest way. The other fairies followed and some got there just before Ruddy. They kept themselves out of sight.

Glow and Starlight made themselves transparent. All Rug could see was Ruddy flying just before she landed. The surprise, in the way she came, was something words could not explain.

He had never seen a Mouhume come from out of the sky before. Rug and his follower looked at each other and went onto their knees bowing their heads. This would be a tale that no other could live up to.

Ruddy had her hand on the handle of her sharp thorn, ready to strike if needed but to her surprise Rug was full of apologies. He told her that he had acted wrong, made so many mistakes and needed guidance. He wanted Tube and Ratty and any other leaders to help him.

She knew by his stance and how he asked for help that he was telling the truth. If he had been there for any other reason he would have more than one Mouhume with him. In fact, he should have had more with him on an ordinary outing. She found that, in itself, strange.

Time was getting on and they weren't under any covering. This is not something what you would say out in the open but ideally they needed to be somewhere that would hide them from view.

The fairies that had hidden themselves flew off after having a quick look around. They could see no danger so reported back to Ruddy but they were still out of sight. Not even Ruddy could see them but she had started to learn their ways: a little tap on her shoulder or a whisper in her ear. She would take Rug and his companion to a garden not that far away from her home but far enough away that the fairies would know if they had visitors.

The Mouhumes journey

Tube and Ratty landed Rug was clearly happy to see them. He started to tell them about his new home whilst the Mouhume he was with went to fill their water pouches up. He told them all how he had made a big mistake.

He also told them how he had gone back to the park and those who had been too weak were now in good health. They had more than enough food and they understood that it had to be stored away in case of poor weather.

It was Ratty who explained to Rug about the strain of what had happened and the lack of food. That had been the main reason why tension had made everyone act out of character at that time.

They showed Rug their new home. Tilly went back home with the help of Glow and Starlight to open the gate. Tube kept quiet about the dogs and the fairies. At this time it was not essential to say anything so none of the Mouhumes from the shed camp said a word unless they were asked.

His head had enough to take in, what with finding them and telling them about his own adventures. So asking about things like the dogs and the fairies with Woozy at this time was not top of his agenda. Some things he even doubted. Had he seen them really or was it some sort of hallucination?

Rug stayed the rest of the day with Tube and Ratty exchanging accounts of what they had seen and difficulties they had to overcome. What had once been one big community was now split into three. Other Mouhumes who had been made to go in another direction might have made another home, unaware that Tube had escaped from danger and now they were all in different locations.

Tube and Rug had both thought of this. They also talked about one day they would like to send out a search party to locate any Mouhumes that might have been split up. They sat for a long time talking about that more than anything else. How long would it take? How many would have to go from each camp and their food supplies?

It was time to go. Rug gave Tube and Ratty a big hug. He was so happy. In the next few days they come back and forth, to each other's camp and even to the park. All of them were now happy about where they were living.

Chapter 15
Lights

IT HAD NOT been that long ago when Jack had put traps around the garden near the pond and in the greenhouse, he had placed most of them around the pond, some down the garden path and some around the hedging leading up the garden. In fact, any place that a small animal might use as cover.

The one in the greenhouse had killed one of the Mouhumes. They had tried to get his body out but the trap was too strong for them. Jack had found it but just picked it up looked strangely at it and then buried it around the back of the greenhouse.

The Mouhumes, knowing how dangerous these traps where, set each trap off with sticks then took the food that had been placed in them

They now had garden lights that turned on as soon as it went dark. This made it more difficult for those who went out on a night time hunting spree. After a few days had passed, they got used to the lights and just went about their jobs as normal.

As they carried on doing what they needed to they took no notice of Jack in his chair looking out. He sat there most times throughout the night and day, hardly ever coming into the garden so they saw him as no danger.

The grass was starting to get long. Ted, next door, kept his grass short. Most gardens had short grass, just one or two let nature take its course.

In a way the long grass gave them some cover. Some of the Mouhumes from the park group were coming. They were going to show them how to fish. The Mouhumes had already tried fishing in their garden but it was more luck than skill if and when they got anything.

It was a full moon and the lights around the pond gave them plenty of light. The park Mouhumes had watched the human's fish and tried to copy them. They might not have had fishing rods but they made do with what they could find and became quite good at fishing.

In the garden the Mouhumes would turn the mice and rat traps over and go onto the water using them as rafts. This was a good way to go onto the water. The park Mouhumes had never used a raft before so this was new to them but their fishing skills were outstanding. They no sooner got out on to the water and started fishing when they pulled a fish out of the water.

Some of the Mouhumes had flowers on top of their head. This helped with camouflaging. They mostly had dandelion flowers on their heads but almost anything would do, depending on what area they were in.

At this time Jack was looking out the window. The Mouhumes took no notice. They knew he was there and that he was not to be feared. He was harmless, apart from setting the traps.

It was good that the lights attracted insects such as moths and other flying bugs. The Mouhumes could, if not for themselves, use them as bait to catch other food stuff like fish and mice. Birds would often fall prey to the traps when the Mouhumes used insects as bait.

The lights had been there for only two nights but the Mouhumes took advantage of this. Even the hedgehog came in after the insects the Mouhumes had put out for him. Glow asked the hedgehog if he would stop going to Buster's garden as he was getting hurt by the thorns coming out of him.

The hedgehog explained why he went to see Buster. The reason was that Buster did not hurt him but helped to get any loose quills out. It was hard to find a way to get them out. Buster rolled him by shoving his face onto him and patting him using his paw which helped to pull the quills out. They needed to be removed so that new ones could grow.

The Mouhumes said that they would be more than happy to take them out for the hedgehogs, because they could be used to help protect them. The quills were long and strong and if they needed to be shorter they could be cut easily.

Once again it had been Ruddy who had made the connection between the two creatures. Something else the community would talk about. It was amazing how she could bring two different worlds together. They worked hard so they could all benefit.

She had made friends with the fairies, Buster, Tilly and now with the hedgehog. Her personality just shone. That was why all the Mouhumes loved her. She would fight without fear to help another Mouhume and even her new friends.

It was Starlight who noticed that Jack was looking a bit flustered. Jack's wife was standing next to him. She looked as if she was laughing. What could have made Jack so restless? He was pacing the floor and going in and out of one room to the next.

Starlight pointed this out to Glow. The two of them went to the window to see if they could hear anything. It became clear that Jack was not happy that a fish had been pulled out from the pond.

They flew back to the pond to tell those that were there to go, to leave quickly as Jack was not happy. The lights had been put there to watch them. Their faces were that of disappointment. They had just thought of Jack as there, nothing more. Just there doing no harm but he was watching them.

In a split second nothing was to be seen. They had all gone back to the shed. Some were in the shed, in a doorway they had made with the help of the fairies. That was something else the fairies were good at, making things.

Some of the Mouhumes went under the shed into the hideaway in the burrow. The shed was a perfect place to hold a meeting. It was all but empty. Some drawers were near the main doorway and there were bits of tools lying around but the floor space was almost clear.

In here it could hold a large number of Mouhumes. It was dry so they would use that for any meetings, if and when it was needed. A large space and the drawers were a good place to stand on. They were above everyone else and he or she could be seen and heard.

The safety of the community was now in question. Why had Jack put lights up? If it had not been for Starlight and Glow they would have never known that Jack was upset about the fish.

The traps also came up in the debate. Why had he put them out with food? When the food was taken it killed the taker!

These were all reasonable questions. Nobody could answer in a positive way. Starlight did not want any harm to come to any of the Mouhumes. She came up with an idea. The fairies would, in turn, watch Jack and his wife, Annie, listening to what was being said. Each day they would report back to Tube for him so he could decide what might be best.

Starlight did not like the idea of Woozy and her being parted. She was willing to do anything to keep them together. She also knew that Glow had a good friendship with Ruddy; she also would not want that to be ended.

Glow, at that time, went back to her community. There were more fairies than Mouhumes so there was more than enough to help spy on Jack to see what he was preparing. Was he out to hurt the Mouhumes or not? The Mouhumes agreed with Starlight they would give it another day or so to see Jack's intentions.

Two fairies, at a time, went to the conservatory where Jack spent most of his time. They would listen to what was being said. When they were relieved from their positions they reported back to Tube and two other senior fairies.

This went on all night, as long as Jack was sitting there with Annie talking. The fairies moved around the roof of the conservatory taking in everything that was talked about, some of the things they had no idea about.

The next day they would have to try to explain to Ted their concerns. For long enough they had tried to communicate with Ted but he could just not understand. This time he was needed, to see what and if he could stop Jack's bad intentions with the Mouhumes.

They had to observe tonight. This was new to them. They had nothing to do with humans apart from Ted. Not even Ted's wife had seen them. They were reluctant to let anyone or anything see them. They had too many bad experiences so they found it was best just to hide away until now. Since the Mouhumes came they had let Buster and Tilly see them, even the hedgehog was now in the group.

This got the fairies colony worried where it might be leading. They had never been seen by humans or any other creatures and all of a sudden they were socializing with allsorts.

Some had made it clear in meetings they started to doubt things, things that where now putting them in danger. They would still help for now, just in case they were wrong. A big if! Looking at all that had gone on. They would look as if they were doing all they could to help the Mouhumes.

Some were ready to go to their own world but even that had been compromised due to the fact that Ruddy had been shown it just before she had her baby. So all they could do was gather evidence all night and see what the next day would bring before they would decide what to do.

Two of the fairies crept in one of the bedroom windows that were open ever so slightly. It was just enough room for them to squeeze in. They heard Jack and Annie coming up the stairs, Annie laughing as she came up.

The fairies hid on the curtain, blending in with the patterns. Jack and Annie got themselves into bed. Annie, now and again, burst into laughter about the look on Jack's face when the Mouhume pulled the fish out of the water.

Just as things went quiet Annie would start laughing. Jack telling her to stop, this went on almost all night: in a way that was a good thing, as the fairies could get a better understanding of Jack and Annie.

This would be something they would report back: Annie found it amusing whilst Jack was upset that one of his fish had been taken. In their opinion, Jack and Annie were not at all bad humans. They cared for the creatures in their garden but would they care for the Mouhumes the same way?

The streetlight was glowing through the curtains. The two fairies were still hidden in the design. They took it in turns to fly around the room looking around to see what they could see trying to find out what sort of people Jack and Annie were.

After nearly being seen a number of times each, they decided to go but not the way they had came in. They decided to go downstairs and look around the rooms.

They had a good look around. There was nothing they could see nothing out of the ordinary but now they would have to find a way out. They checked the windows in the living room but they were all locked.

Even the window at the bottom of the staircase was locked. They started to get worried as they could hear movement from upstairs. They flew into the kitchen area but the windows in there were also locked.

They were now in need of energy. One of the windows in the kitchen area looked into the conservatory. As they looked through the glass they could see that one of the windows was slightly open, the catch had not been put down properly. Maybe due to Jack and Annie going to bed laughing and otherwise distracted they had forgotten to close it.

The door that led into the conservatory was slightly open. Though not big enough for them to squeeze through but maybe they could pull it open? These two fairies were smaller than most, they were not as strong as the others and now they did not have sufficient amount of energy to blend into the background.

As they tried to pull the door open they could hear footsteps upstairs and the creaking of the floorboards. They were starting to get worried that they might be seen.

Some Mouhumes had seen them trying to pull the door open but how could they help? It would be almost impossible to help! They stood watching thinking about what they could do. After what had happened to Jumper, Ruddy and the others it had been forbidden for any Mouhume to enter into a human's house.

It was early morning so finding a fairy would be hard to do. Even in the daylight, if they did not want to be seen, they would have no chance. One of the Mouhumes had some twine but could he throw it high enough so they could scale the height they would need?

No matter what they did they could not get the twine anywhere high enough. A number of Mouhumes were looking to see if they could find a fairy. As it was still early they would not even be at the bush were they recharged in daylight?

The fairies in the house had been resting all day. That was why they had been chosen to watch Jack and Annie that night but they had misjudged how much energy they had used.

One of the Mouhumes had an idea. In Jack's garden was a cherry tree. One of the branches had been sawn off by Jack the year before and it was trickling out sap, sticky sap. The Mouhume got some flower heads and filled them with sap. It had to work he passed them onto other Mouhumes who carried the flower heads up towards the conservatory.

Time was against them. Even outside they could hear movement upstairs. What they did next was nothing they had seen done before, but they had to do something. Some of the Mouhumes climbed onto the outside window ledge. The flower heads were passed up; the Mouhumes on the window ledge then got handfuls and threw it on to both the window and onto the white plastic frame. Then, in turns, with hands full of sap they attempted to scale up the window but they just slid back down again.

The plastic frame seemed to have had a better hold. They took it in turns as soon as they got so far up they slid back down. But each time they were getting a little higher until finally they reached the window that was slightly open.

The twine was passed up and attached to a screw holding the guttering. Four Mouhumes with clean hands ascended up the side of the conservatory. It took two of them to pull the window open.

Once it was open they attached some more string and climbed down. There were four of them in the human's house with panic in their hearts. It was not just for the fact that if they were found by the humans but the fact was what would happen when Tube found out.

They rushed to the door. Now the two fairies where lying on the floor, plain to be seen by all. They had used all their energy. By luck and luck alone they were smaller than most fairies.

Two of the Mouhumes picked up one each and put them over their shoulder and with a Mouhume behind taking some weight they climbed the twine passing the fairies down to the other Mouhumes who were waiting.

The Mouhumes had to scale down the outside with their feet that were now covered with a little fur from their clothing, wiping away the sap. The last one undoing the string and making the final descent using all his body hoping to clean away any last marks, hoping he was not going to fall to a certain death. Luckily as he fell, the fur from his clothes clung to the sticky sap. Not all the evidence was wiped away but they had no more time, a dark streak was now left on the white plastic.

As the Mouhumes ran to hide they heard Jack in the conservatory. They were still in sight but hoped they had not been seen. Some went next door to put the fairies near the energizing bush, before they eventually all returned to the shed.

Chapter 16
The Gathering

THE NEXT DAY was the strangest yet! Some Mouhumes stayed near the pond. Hiding in the shrubbery watching the room where Jack sat looking out. That morning he had only stayed in the room a short time.

The fairies that had been in the house were still weak so not much was asked of them. The Mouhumes who had gone in the house and those who helped them were now being questioned. They knew they would be in trouble and there was one punishment that they dreaded and that was to be expelled from the Mouhume communities.

It had only happened once to their knowledge, back in the old home. Five Mouhumes had gone into a house and had been seen. That, in turn, put the whole community in danger so they were banished never to return.

The five had been going into a house where an elderly human lived. They thought they were helping, by doing little jobs such as helping to stitch anything that needed stitching and cleaning up around the rooms.

One day, however, the human set a trap and tried to follow them back home. They had discovered that by stopping for a rest, as the day had been hot, they had left footprints: on the bottom of their feet was white dust.

The human had kept his distance but they had seen the human hiding behind a bush so they had to change direction. For days after the human kept going there, looking around and hoping to find them.

What had been a good deed had confined them to camp for days. Only Mouhumes keeping watch were out, the rest hidden away in camp until the human stopped looking for them. The stress they had been under was something they never wanted again.

The odd Mouhume still went into houses but never took anything or helped in any way so that humans wouldn't know they had visitors. This was different, Jack had seen them and they had seen Jack. Right up until he saw them fishing, the two worlds just got on doing their own thing.

It was later that day the fairies held the gathering in the big shed. They reported what they had seen and what they had heard. They also thanked the Mouhumes for helping them get out of the house.

Tube sat with a stern look but never said anything. He knew what they had done was brave. He had been up the garden and he had seen there was a number of tell tale signs.

The only thing was, had Jack seen the tell tale signs? It had been reported back to Tube that Jack and Annie had left in the car some time ago. Tube had asked Glow and Starlight if they could help clean the mess on the side of the white wall.

They agreed but it took some time. The Mouhumes could not do a lot as the window was now closed. They could not even fasten the cord. They had not seen the screw the Mouhumes had tied onto the night before.

So the fairies cleaned up for them and now it was the fairies who had called the meeting. They were unhappy about everything that had been happening: dogs, hedgehogs and the coming and goings of Mouhumes from different camps.

The fairies were concerned about their own well-being. They felt the Mouhumes had not done anything but bring potential danger to their door.

They were open about each concern and explaining why: the hedgehogs eat insects, worms, and any other meat they can get a hold of including dragonflies. Which were part of the fairy family but not yet evolved.

Not even the best Mouhume could defend themselves against a hedgehog. If the hedgehog wanted to harm them they easily could. At this time they did not need to harm the Mouhumes as the Mouhumes were feeding them but if food was to run short they would, without hesitation, feed themselves on whatever was around at that time.

Tube looked worried about what was being said. He had the same thoughts himself when they discovered that fairies were close to them. He could understand the concern the fairies had. The last few days had been nothing but discovery. They were opening worlds that would normally avoid each other.

Every concern was opened and each one was put to discussion. In each case it was the fairies that had the worry and it was the fairies that had lived in harmony with humans.

Although the fairies did say in their defence, it was only Ted that they had made contact with, not even Ted's wife had ever seen them and they had lived alongside them for a number of years.

The only contact they made with other creatures was only when needed. If it had not been for Ruddy and Capheus, contact between the Mouhumes and the fairies would not have happened and if not for the Mouhumes, the two dogs Buster and Tilly, would not be aware of the fairy world.

It all came back to Ruddy: her inquisitive ways, wanting to explore all aspects of the surrounding areas and her fearless and reckless ways were, once again, being questioned. All Glow wanted to know was whether the Mouhumes would stop letting other creatures into their world and stop letting others knowing they even existed?

Tube nodded. He knew they were right again. Then came another truth. It had been all one-sided. The fairy community had been helping the Mouhumes with anything they could not do themselves and at the same time putting their own health at risk. They had asked for nothing in return but now it had to stop.

The shed was almost full of the Mouhumes. Glow was putting up a good argument just her and four other fairies. Glow was around the same size as a Mouhume in height, two others were half the size but the one standing out of sight was bigger than Starlight. What ever war wounds Glow had, this fairy had more. With just one look at her you could tell that she was fearless and stronger than any other fairy.

They said what they would like from the Mouhumes and that was for the Mouhumes to stop letting anything and everything know about the fairies, it was not a lot to ask!

Tube had not let the woodland Mouhumes know about the fairies and he had not let the parkland Mouhumes know. As far as he was aware they still did not know but they were right the dogs now knew and the hedgehog knew.

He agreed without putting up any debate. He then told the Mouhumes the two fairies had reported back and that as far as they knew the humans, Jack and Annie, seemed to care about some of the creatures in the garden, more than others.

At this time they would have to try and hide away and keep out of sight until they knew what would happen next. He reminded them the last few times Jack had not been sitting in the window. He had come back with things that could be, in all probability, a danger to the Mouhumes. Things like the rat trap and the lights.

Just as Tube was about to say something else a Mouhume came running in and reported that there were now three humans sitting looking out of the window. When asked what they were doing he was told just sitting looking out.

Tube looked at Glow but did not say a word. This was something he needed to know but he also knew that Glow was right. The Mouhumes had done nothing for them except bring them nothing but danger.

Glow had not seen Tube look at her with want in his eyes. She had her back to him. She was talking to her friends and then they were off.

It was now evening the light was dull. It had been a long discussion and now it was time to get food, after all they were now under the cover of darkness. The fairy community would now be out of sight. Darkness was not a friend of theirs. It wore them out, as those two fairies the night before had found out.

Tube wanted to go up the garden and see what was happening. He wanted to know who was sitting looking out the window. There was around six Mouhumes there already. They could not understand what was being said but they might have some idea just watching.

The Mouhumes went about their business, collecting food and other stuff. One or two of them were watching Jack and Annie and this new human. The humans were watching them. Now and again the humans were getting up and going into another room adjoining the conservatory.

It was clear to see they were talking and sometimes pointing towards where the Mouhumes were. As daylight came the Mouhumes finally went back under the shed to rest. Only a small number of Mouhumes stayed out in daylight.

Those in the conservatory went so the area was now clear. That day they did not see Jack or Annie. The car that had brought the other human had also gone. The Mouhumes now knew how dependent they had been on the fairies and how much they needed their help to understand what was being said.

The rest of the day was as normal as it could be. The fairies kept themselves to themselves, as did the Mouhumes.

Chapter 17
Quiet Days

THE NEXT TWO days the Mouhumes and fairies did not see one another. The fairy world could keep out of sight but still watch the Mouhumes. They watched the Mouhumes trying to communicate with other creatures they could not understand.

The fairies wanted the Mouhumes to see how much they needed them. Buster and Tilly, as friendly as they were with the Mouhumes, lost that connection due to not understanding what the other wanted.

The fairies would normally translate for them but now they had lost that and had to find another way to understand each other. That was not a bad thing as they were starting to depend on the fairies more and more. Now they had to do what they had always done and that was to learn fast about the world they had not just discovered but made for themselves.

Ruddy was trying to make friends with the kitten that belonged to Ted. She knew that if she could not make friends with it as it got bigger it would be a deadly enemy. She gave herself a week to have it as a friend or she would have to try and kill it.

The kitten grew bigger each day; it was exploring the area with more and more interest. It was looking into every corner whilst on the prowl. At this time it was still playful but Ruddy knew it would only be a matter of time before instinct would kick in and it would be killing. She had a son to take care of so she wanted to keep her distance from any danger that might come near. So making friends with it was one way.

Glow and other fairies stayed out of sight watching all the time to see the true Mouhume and to see if they had any other ideas. They watched Ruddy the most, as she was the fearless one. They wanted to know if it was right what some Mouhumes had said, unaware they were being listened to. She was a killing phenomenon they would say. She killed anything in her way without hesitation no matter what.

There were parts Glow had seen: her reaction, her speed and her strength but that was not all of Ruddy. She had something else. Something she had not seen in her own kind. She had a want to get along with others but some did not see this. They had put her upon a high platform so no matter what she did she would be liked or disliked.

Glow could not believe herself. She had almost blamed Ruddy for the mishaps as Ruddy was the only common denominator in all those so called friendships or those who had been enemies, such as Rug.

Ruddy was teaching her son Dash how to catch a bird, what size it should be and so on. It was the same with fishing: it was no good trying to catch a fish that was as big as them because it would pull them into the water. That was something a Mouhume would never survive as a Mouhume could not swim. They had no ponds or lakes where they had lived.

The fairies had little time for birds as birds often went after fairies to kill and eat them. The fairies had little hope against a bird on ground or in the air, no matter what size the bird was.

Whilst the Mouhumes where being watched the fairies had seen that a small number from this community were going to the woodlands community and also to the parklands. They had all started to keep in contact with each other on a daily basis. This was good to know. It gave the Mouhumes strength in numbers if needed. The Mouhumes had no idea how many fairy communities there were. This was something fairies did not want to share.

Dash was distracted. His mother was crouching down behind a flowering shrub ready to attack a bird when he went to look in the pond, something had caught his eye. He was standing on the edge of the paving stones that went around the pond, surrounded by a border with flowers and plants. Dash was bending over the edge looking into the water when something knocked him in. A toad, it had been startled and jumped out from behind the plants around the pond.

Dash yelled for help but Ruddy was now in conflict with a bird and she would be the only Mouhume close enough that would put her life at risk for another.

Starlight heard and without hesitation she was at the pond trying to pull out Dash. At this time Ruddy had seen what was happening and quickly was on her way. Starlight's wings got soaked as she pulled Dash out from the water. Now she was in need of help as she could not open her wings as wide as she would have liked and was struggling to get on the path around the pond. She got as near to the edge as she could but her

The Mouhumes journey

wings were now weighing her down and the clothing Dash had on was pulling the two of them down.

Then a hand grabbed hold of the two of them trying desperately to pull them out. It was Mousey holding onto them at the same time. His body was leaning backwards holding on to the two of them. Their heads were now just above the water.

The fish swimming below were taking a nibble at their feet but not getting a hold properly. Each time though it was pulling them back under the water and each time almost pulling Mousey in too.

Glow arrived and could see this, quickly she pulled out Starlight. She dropped her onto the dry path and then back to pull out Dash at which time Ruddy had landed too.

It had all happened in a moment. Starlight was like a wet rag as was Dash. The two of them were on the dry path lying in a pool of water. Ruddy seeing to her son whilst Mousey and Glow saw to Starlight. What a day it had been, once again, the fairies put their own well-being at risk to save a Mouhume.

Mousey was a hero that day, not just in the eyes of the Mouhumes but the fairies also thought of him as a friend. He could have let go anytime as he too was in danger, in danger of also being pulled in but he had held on to the two of them, not favouring one more than the other.

Celebrations were cut short when the man who had been there the other day talking to Jack and Annie came back. That had been when the dead Mouhume was dug up from the back of the shed. This was alarming for the Mouhumes and they needed to know why? So what they did was to get Ted to go and see but as none of them could speak to Ted, not even the fairies, how could they get him to go around to Jack's house?

Ted had some plant pots with soil in them but nothing planted in them. It was just dry soil. So the Mouhumes wanted a sign for Ted to see. They started to empty the soil from the pots just by picking it out by hand or anything that could scoop it out then they threw it onto the patio. When there was enough they spread it like a fine dust then they used their feet to make an arrow-like mark pointing to Jack's house.

The fairies would have to get Ted's attention. There was only one way they could do that. Ted had a bell on the outside wall; this was for the fairies when they needed Ted. They would swing on the string until it rang. Ted being a little hard of hearing now sometimes took longer than other times.

They rang it hard and fast until Ted came out. They waved at him to follow them around the back garden then they pointed to the ground with the arrow. Flying over the hedge they waved for him to follow. Ted went as quickly as his old legs could carry him around the front then straight into Jack's kitchen. There were voices louder than normal coming from Jack's house.

Ted came out. He was only in Jack's house for a short time. The fairies could not hear what had been said so could not tell the Mouhumes anything. The plan was for one fairy to follow Ted into Jack's house but Ted shut the door behind him as he went in.

They would have to wait and hope that Ted would tell them but Ted sometimes just thought they would know about things so he would not say anything. Not just that but anyone watching or listening might think that he was talking to himself. He was always conscious of that. His wife Linda had often found him talking to himself and would give a comment about him talking to himself but in reality he was talking to the fairies.

There was no news so they would just have to wait to see what the outcome might be. There was one thing that was learnt that day: both sides helped one another without thinking.

It was near the end of the day and the darkness was cutting in. They parted as normal. The Mouhumes knew that most of the fairies needed to settle down at night, although some still had enough energy until early morning. Tube understood this and knew that this would be something he would have done if he was the leader of the fairy colony.

The Mouhumes returned to the sheds they held discussions about what had gone on with the fairies and the human called Ted, Tube listened but one thing kept making him laugh was Mousey's story about being thrown away. When, in fact, he had been pulled out of harm's way and had passed out in shock.

Mousey's explanation was, that his mind was going that fast he could foresee it and only days earlier Ruddy had been dropped from a great height so it was not far from being the truth. It could have happened!

It was only later, after he passed out, he found himself in the outhouse. He woke up to find Ruddy standing over him but she was looking poorly.

Then a fairy came to in to see if we were better. Then I was told about what I had done: I had unknowingly walked into the resting area of the fairies that needed re-energizing from the sunrays. That's what they do, they re-energize from the sun, two or three times a day.

That's also how they can hide. They imitate what they are near, making it almost impossible to see them.

Mousey went on with many more interesting accounts of what he now knew. Even telling Scallop what he had learned in the short time he was with the fairy called Glow.

It was a lot to take in for Tube and Ratty and some of the other leaders. Why would they tell others of their weakness? What would they benefit from it? They had no idea who the Mouhumes were, so why tell them?

Ruddy was next telling them of her account. How she sensed something behind her, how she was taken into the air with a vice-like grip. No matter how hard she tried to break loose she could not. Then she was dropped but it was no ordinary drop, she was spun so that she could not do anything to help herself.

Then the next thing she was saved by Capheus. "He was injured by helping me. I felt under the weather after that and that was why I went out of the way from everyone anyway. The next day I went to see what these creatures were."

"It took time but then they showed themselves and took me somewhere. All I remember was that I was shown some place that I could not describe and colours that I have never seen before and could not even explain what they might look like. Things were there but not really there. It was all too much then I passed out. The next thing I knew I was with baby and they took care of me until you came for me."

Tube and Ratty were astonished. Mixing with other creatures and getting help from outside was not the Mouhume way. Though, if they wanted to stay there they would have to try and work together and the way forward was with Ruddy, Mousey and Scallop. As it was now these three who had the most contact with the fairy world.

Chapter 18
Buster

It was Ruddy who seemed to be the bond between the two different worlds. It took no time for her to be back on her feet. Her baby was now walking. She had plenty to show him. Dash she called him and he was just like his father, Jumper, in so many ways. She had seen no reason to live after he was killed, that was why she had attacked everything in her way but it was different now. She had a son who depended on her.

A few days earlier she had even took him to see Buster and Tilly. They loved him. Tilly let him sit on her back and hold onto the fur around her neck, not that she had much loose fur, so sometimes he would hold onto her ears.

Buster was Ruddy's friend. Sometimes Glow would come and spend time with them. She could talk to both of them and she would be the intermediate between the two. This helped the two dogs get to know them. Ruddy tried to go to see Buster and Tilly every day but sometimes their human would be there so she would have to stay hidden in the shrubbery.

Back in their Garden, Jack would often come into the garden putting out new, or setting the traps back up into different areas of the garden. The Mouhumes were not sure if the traps were set there to hurt them or to prevent other animals from getting the food. After all, the Mouhumes now knew how to set them off without being hurt and then to take the food. They thought that Jack must be like Ted. Ted looked out for the fairies.

Some of the Mouhumes were around the pond. They could hear talking from next door, so they popped their heads through or around the hedge to see who it was. Ted and Jack were sitting there talking. The Mouhumes could not understand what was being said, they looked around the garden to see if any of the fairies were there but they could not see any so they went back to the pond.

The pond had lots of different plants growing in and around it. There was a good covering to hide amongst and a waterfall which came out of a castle. It attracted all sorts of creatures: toads, frogs, newts, dragonflies and even a grass snake. The birds would swoop down for a drink. The pond itself was a haven for most wildlife or so it would seem.

Ruddy was showing Dash around the pond. She needed to show him all the different creatures that lived around the pond. She did not want what had happened days earlier to happen again some of the other Mouhumes were also there collecting insects, another good source of food for them. It gave them protein and that, along with other foods they were now having, it helped them survive that much better.

Ruddy was going in and out the plants showing Dash the way up to the waterfall. It had rocks and plants growing all the way up, almost hiding the castle walls. It was a wonderful sight for man or creature.

Next door Ted was with Jack having drinks and chatting about all sorts of things. The fairies were hiding out of sight. One or two were now near Ruddy, showing themselves now and again, as if they were playing hide and seek.

Everything was peaceful. There was nothing to fear or to be concerned about. There was only the slightest breeze that was barely moving the leaves on the plants. You could hear the sound of the waterfall and the birds and chatting that came from next door.

So this would be a good time to show Dash around the pond. She showed him the little hiding holes, the top of the castle where the water came down from and the collection of water at the top that housed frogs and toads and newts. It formed a pool then it overflowed down into the big pond where the fish lived and the dragonflies would swoop down for a drink or insects.

Glow came and tapped Ruddy on the shoulder. This gave her a fright but she was still getting used to her new friends and their ways. Glow started to tell Ruddy that one or two fairies were showing themselves to Jack. Ted had asked them if they would so that he might understand our ways.

Ruddy looked puzzled. Glow was just starting to explain when a slight sound came from the hedge separating the two gardens. It was Ted's kitten, a tabby cat and it had mischief in mind. The cat with its sleekness went through the hedge, scarcely making a sound, slowly creeping towards the pond.

Another fairy had seen what was going to happen so came to inform Glow. Glow told Ruddy to hide as soon as possible which she did.

Ruddy placed her body in front of Dash, protecting her son holding her thorn in her hand ready to strike. Glow and the other fairy flew off, informing the rest of the Mouhumes who were at the pond. They were off leaving Ruddy and Dash. There was nothing they could do with this young cat.

The Mouhumes ran through the top of the gardens heading to the only safe place that Glow told them about. The other fairy, just above them, told them what she needed them to do. She was bigger than Glow and full of colours, you could easy mistake her for a flower. She was called Bouquet. She could blend in with most flowers, making her almost invisible and that was without using her ability of disappearing.

Glow flew down to where Buster lived. He was, as normal, sniffing in the flower area looking for what ever he could find. Tilly was pulling at a rope hanging from a tree, this was how she played, pulling and tugging at the rope. Glow went straight over to Buster and told him that Ruddy and Dash were in need of his help straight away. Then Glow flew over to the gate. It had some heavy rope over the top of the gate which also looped over the fence post.

Glow pulled hard at the rope trying to loosen it but it was harder than she thought. Buster also used his muzzle under the rope at the post end along with Glow. Eventually they got it off. Then Glow pulled the gate open, just enough for Buster to put his nose in between the gate and the fence post, pushing it open.

Buster ran up the street towards Jack's house. When he got there, the gate to Jacks garden was almost open. Bouquet and one of the other Mouhumes were trying hard to get it open for Buster.

Bouquet had opened the catch on the gate, the Mouhume holding the string that Bouquet had tied on the gate and was pulling it open with all his might. Buster, the same as before, opened it with his head and followed the fairy to where Ruddy was.

Glow returned to where Ruddy was. The kitten had not found her yet but had found a toad that had just jumped onto a Lilly pad with a beautiful yellow flower. The toad sat very still, watching as if it knew the kitten could not reach it.

Buster came around the pond like a bull in a china shop putting his head into the plants even though he was not really sure what he was looking for. The kitten, as quietly as it came, turned around and quickly went the same way back home.

Buster was still poking his head into the plants and rustling through them. Suddenly he found what he was looking for. Ruddy came out of her hiding hole with Dash. Ruddy rubbed Buster's nose and thanked him.

Then suddenly they heard shouting. Jack came around to the pond with a brush that had been at the side of the house. He poked Buster with the brush end, almost knocking him into the pond. Buster put his head down, and his tail high up in the air, wagging it. He started to bark at Jack. Jack again pushed the brush into Buster. Buster grabbed hold of the brush shank. Then with his strong jaws he snapped it. Jack fell backwards on to the fence. Lucky for him the fence kept him up. Buster jumped up at him putting Jack's hand into his mouth. Jack almost passed out. Buster then put his front paws back onto the ground letting go of Jack's hand he then licked it, to Jack's surprise.

Jack started to stroke Buster. Buster loved getting all this attention. Then he heard his mistress calling for him. Kez his owner had heard Buster bark so came looking for him to see what he was up to. She explained to Jack that he was a friendly dog. As they stood talking, Annie arrived home. Buster got even more attention. Kez then said that she would have to go back home as Tilly had got out as well. So she called for Buster who followed her back home.

Chapter 19
The First Meeting

THE MOUHUMES HAD all gone back to under the shed. A lot had happened. Tube was now wondering if staying there was a good idea. Yes they might have good allies in the fairies but they seemed to be finding trouble every day.

Ratty came to see Tube: he could see that he was troubled. He also had an idea what it would be about. All this new stuff was a lot to take in. Ratty had also thought was it worth while?

All they had to put up with in their last home was second nature. Yes it would have to be a gathering but Ratty had made his mind up he was going to leave. Some others had also made their minds up. Not just from this camp but from the woodland and the parkland camps too. Some from those two camps wanted to move on and getaway from the humans.

So before Tube could say anything Ratty told him that he was going to leave. He had no idea where he was going but in a weeks' time he and some others were going to go to find, a place away from humans.

Tube was disappointed Ratty had already arranged to go without telling him. They had been friends from a young age. They had helped each other countless times and now Ratty wanted to go by himself.

Tube nodded as if to say he understood but the look on his face was that of sadness and disappointment. Ratty saw this and was quick to tell him that he wanted the both of them to leave and set up elsewhere. Tube could not hide his delight, he smiled from ear to ear and gave Ratty a "never before" big hug.

Tube hardly ever, if not never, showed his emotion to another but this was a big thing. Another adventure with new, exciting discoveries and what could be better than doing it with a companion that you had shared all your experiences with.

They sat talking in the chamber under the shed trying to work out how and when they would inform the others to see who wanted to come with them and who wanted to stay. Then they had to discuss the food supplies: what they could take and what they would leave.

Ratty told Tube that most of the food was already worked out, depending on how many were staying and leaving. It had been a week or two ago that Ratty had decided to go: he had been gathering and collecting food and hunting equipment.

Tube was taken aback with all this, how had he not noticed? All this was happening with his best friend and he had not seen any signs. Ratty started to tell him there had been a lot going on and with Tube being the leader he had not wanted to burden him with anything else so he had corresponded with the other two camps.

It was not going to be something that was ... he stopped he could not explain what he meant. It was not going to be something like sneaking out of camp with food provisions and the rest waking up to half the camp gone.

As they were talking a young Mouhume came to inform them that Jack was looking round the back of the sheds. He was in the greenhouse then at the back of the sheds then back in the greenhouse and then back around the sheds.

What could he be looking for? The Mouhume then told Tube that Jack had just gone back towards the house. What could they do? What should they do? Tube told all the Mouhumes to stay under the shed and to be ready at the escape exits.

They asked if they had to escape where should they go? What direction they should take? How many should there be in each group? They could not all run in the same direction as it would be easy for any enemy to see them. That was why they needed different escape routes so they could travel in different directions. It might take longer than other routes but it would be safer for all to do it that way.

Ratty and Tube hid under the shed listening for any sound that might be a human. The sky had gone dark: big black clouds had filled the sky. It was going to rain and rain hard. Tube could tell from the smell in the air. It was going to be a night that no Mouhume could travel.

Then he heard Jack and Annie coming down the path talking quietly. The shed door was being forced opened. There was a loud cracking sound as if something had been broken. It was the door, it had not been opened for a long time and the hinge had rusted. Then the sound of drawers being opened and shut was heard, what could he be doing? Then they heard footsteps going back up the garden.

They must have given up, Tube thought. So Tube went into the shed from the side where they had made a doorway of their own. As he crept in he could see a silhouette at the doorway. He could tell that it was Jack from the outline. He was not moving just standing in one place as still as a statue. What could he be doing Tube thought? Ratty was just about to come into the shed the same way as Tube did but Tube stopped him.

More footsteps were hurrying down the garden. Tube was now getting worried. He had no idea what was going to happen. They then turned a bright light on. Tube had never been this close to a bright light being shined into his eyes before. He could not adjust to the bright light; he just flopped to the floor rubbing his eyes. The light was being moved around the shed to lighten up different areas. Ratty could see a light was being shone inside the shed from the breaks in the floor.

Ratty was worried for his friend Tube, what was happening? Dare he open the door to see what was happening? He stood listening. He could hear Jack talk to Annie but he could not understand what was being said. He heard something being moved; maybe it was being picked up? It sounded like a metal object, the sound of scrapping slightly on the floor.

Tube sat there holding onto some food that he had. He was too frightened to drop it but still looked at Jack not knowing if he should run or stay. He looked around the door that he came in, it was now shut. He had told Ratty to shut it. He looked at the main doorway where Annie and Jack were standing; if he ran he would have to run between their feet. He decided to stay. They had seen him anyway, he was feeling tired and what would be would be!

Jack looked at Annie. He asked her if he should hit it with the trowel. She told him not to. He bent down, Tube closed his eyes; fear was running through his body because he did not know what Jack would do. Jack put the garden trowel near Tube. Tube, at one stage, thought that Jack was going to hit him. Jack gently moved the Trowel under Tube. Tube adjusted himself but was still sitting and still holding onto the food. Jack was now holding Tube up in the air looking at him. So Tube looked back at him. He could see every detail of Jack's face as could Jack see every detail of Tube.

Annie and Jack started to talk to each other. Tube had no idea what they were saying so he had a bite of the food he had, it was no good sitting hungry. Tube had put a lot of weight on lately. He had not needed to hunt like the other Mouhumes. Food at this time was plentiful. It had got darker now and the rain was coming down harder than ever. Jack was turning one way then the other way as if he was going to take Tube out in the rain, then he turned back into the shed. The rain was coming in the doorway wetting Annie and Jack. Rain was hitting the trowel and wetting Tube too. At this point Tube was looking for a way to get off the trowel. If only Jack would keep still but he was turning too fast for Tube to jump.

Tube knew that Jack had seen the fairies at Ted's house. That was one of the reasons why he had not run away when Jack came into the shed but he had still taken a risk. After all, Jack had put out traps that had killed one of the Mouhumes. Jack started to bend down placing the trowel on the floor. Tube stayed there for a little while, not knowing if he should get off or not.

Annie had already gone up the garden and Jack started to follow. He shut the door on his way out. He was not as quick as Annie as he walked up the garden. He got soaked. The Mouhumes under the shed could see this but they did not know Jack was in poor health and was going to get worse with every step. The cold rain was affecting all his joints and bringing with it more pain. By the time Jack got to the top of the garden he had slowed down, his body was now finding it very hard to move.

The Mouhumes under the shed could not see what happened next to Jack and they were not really concerned either. They all came together to talk about what had just happened and that was the only concern they had at this time.

Chapter 20

THE NEXT DAY the rain had stopped. The ground was wet and in some areas soaked with pools of water all over the place. At the back of the shed there was a deep hole that Jack and Annie had dug days earlier now it was full of water. The Mouhumes had no idea why the humans had dug a hole that deep, had it been to try and catch a Mouhume? If a Mouhume had fallen into the hole it would have been hard but not impossible to get out. They had no idea why they would do such a thing, now the clay on the lawn was a right mess! Jack and Annie had dug the hole; they had pulled out some clay and put it on the lawn hoping that what Ted had told them may come true, that they would wake up to an amazing ornament but so far this had not happened. The only thing there was a big mound of mud.

Ratty was told while the talks were taking place in the shed that Jack and Annie's house had blue flashing lights outside. Two Humans had gone into the house and someone had been carried out. They did not know who it was that had been carried out. They were expecting to see Jack or Annie that morning but there was no sign of them, not even in the conservatory.

Ratty was not to worried about this news. He and Tube had other things to attend to and the weather was not something they wanted to be out in. Most of them would be stopping under the shed or in the little shed for cover. The fairies would not be out in this either as their wings would get wet and they would not be able to fly. So Ratty and Tube knew they could not ask them what had happened in the house.

It would be too risky for a Mouhume to go and inspect the house or would it? Ratty had an idea. Would it be a risk as Jack and Annie had seen Tube and not hurt him? It would be an idea to put to Tube. Tube was now back in the shed alone, waiting for Ratty to arrive. They had a lot to talk about this had been something that had kept Tube awake all the night. He wondered if it was the right idea. In a way he had hoped that Jack would hurt him then the decision would have been made for them, from that action alone.

But Jack had not hurt him and this had troubled Tube. If they moved away and came in contact with other humans, would they be the same as Ted, Jack and Annie? The human over the road killed the birds and rabbits by using poison which would then kill any other animal that ate them. That was not a human they would want to come into contacted with.

Tube wondered if there was a place that had no humans or was it just a hope of something better than what they had? He had all these thoughts going through his mind. He knew that Ratty was determined to go away and start again but was there such a place? Tube knew that food here was plentiful. Yes it had risks but so did everywhere. Here they had allies with the fairies, Buster and Tilly. Jack had not hurt him so ... Ratty arrived then so he no longer had time to think of the question what if?

Ratty was full of enthusiasm. The weather outside might have been wet but this had not dampened Ratty's mood. He had a lot to talk about and things to sort out with Tube. Although as he approached Tube he could tell that Tube must have had second thoughts. Tube's face could not hide how he was feeling.

Tube told Ratty what he had been thinking. He told him all the good points and the bad points. He trusted Ratty and his opinion, but this time Ratty was not thinking as he would have normally. This time he was not looking at it as he would have most things that might have a serious outcome for the Mouhumes colony.

Ratty told Tube his thoughts and pointed out the danger if they stayed. If the fairy clan decided to turn on them what could they do? They had no idea how many fairies there were and they could attack without being seen. Ratty had a good point. Tube had talked this over with Ratty many times. They had no idea what or where the fairies went on a night time or when the weather was bad. Yet the fairies knew where the Mouhumes would be almost all of the time.

Tube reminded Ratty the fairies had openly told them almost everything right from the beginning: how they got their energy and strength, how they could do some things but not others and they told them of the weakness that they had. Ratty listened and agreed with most things but then put doubt in when there could be something that might have been misleading:

"Why would another creature tell you all their weaknesses when you have just met them?" Ratty asked "if not only to mislead you or maybe for us to tell them about our weakness"

Tube had talked many a time about this not just with Ratty but other Mouhumes. Each and everyone had always thought the same, that it might be a trap.

Then the truth came out. Ratty thought that if he and others from the park and the woodland left to find a new home and those who had stayed here got attacked by the fairies because the numbers were small then word would get back. They would then know nothing could be trusted again.

Tube's head fell into his chest: his thoughts, his wants, his … it no longer mattered. He would stay with who wanted to stay. Ratty could not go anywhere yet, the weather was not good enough to travel in. It would be the next day he would be more likely to go, if not, the day after that. Tube would help Ratty get everything he needed for the journey. This would be a sad day for the two of them. They had always been near each other side by side in all sorts of adventures.

Ratty had always known that Tube would not go. Tube was looking his age now. Ratty was a little younger but Tube, with all the battles his body had been through, was now showing tell tale signs.

Chapter 21
Strange Happenings

THERE HAD BEEN no sign of Jack in the conservatory, during the day or in the evening, there had been no sign of Annie coming and going throughout the day or night. This got the Mouhumes a little worried about what was happening? The mound of clay on the lawn was still wet with the rain. There was also a ring of yellow mud around it on the grass. It looked terrible.

The weather was getting a little better or at least it had stopped raining. Ratty was making plans to leave the following day. Some of the Parkland Mouhumes and some of the Woodland Mouhumes had come to the shed to make plans: what way would they go? How long do they think the journey would take? They all agreed that word would be sent back to let them know where they were and how they were doing.

There was around twenty or more just from the Parkland. Tube asked them if there was anyone left. They smiled and said there was more than enough left at the park. They were right, at least double were still at the park. They had done well to recover that was done with the help of all the resources around them.

It was late evening before they saw any fairies. The light was dimming. There was still no sign that anyone was in the house. Starlight and eight other fairies were around the muddy area. Tube was under the shed. He had not wanted to go into the shed as the talks had nothing to do with him until they had decided when and where they were going. Instead, he watched what the fairies were doing. They had some paper that had been left days earlier when the mud had been tipped out of the wheelbarrow.

Starlight had picked the paper up it had been left the same time as the mud had been left on the lawn. She had known that it was going to rain but not just that they still had not decided if they were going to do what Jack and Annie wanted. They had needed to wait and see if they deserved what they were asking. By what they had been told from some of the Mouhumes there was sufficient evidence to say that they were good humans. They might have lived next door for a number of years but the fairies had kept out of the way so they did not see a lot of Jack and Annie. And because they had no pets the fairies had no idea if they liked animals.

Yet they had the pond, but this was in question as the fish sometimes tried to eat the fairies if they went for a drink and lately Jack just sat looking out of the window. So they had no idea what sort of humans they were.

The fairies went about what they had started. Tube was amazed with what they had done in such a short time. He had seen nothing like it, not just the speed and work they were doing but it would have taken the Mouhumes twice as long with the same amount of workforce. He had to go and inspect it closer. Starlight heard him coming and grabbed hold of some clay and without a word plonked it on Tube's head then flew on top of the hedge out of his reach laughing. Tube without saying anything or even his facial expression changing just looked at the work that had been done. The detail was like nothing he had seen before not even the best workers in the Mouhumes community could have completed a job like this! Not in the time they had done it and not even if they had longer.

Starlight was surprised that Tube had not said or done anything as she watched from the top of the hedge. She fluttered down beside Tube. Tube, still not making any sort of response, continued looking at the work that Starlight and her friends had done.

She asked was there something wrong. He shook his head then said that it was perfect and that he had never seen or had the capability to have done something that good. He then knew that he and the Mouhumes had so much to learn. Ratty and the others might be leaving too soon. They had so much to learn too. Maybe the fairies were not bad and did not have alternative motives? Maybe they just like to help?

Starlight was now looking around. At the work they had just done, it looked okay so why was Tube still just looking? It was getting dark now so she said her goodbyes. Just as she said this the lights went on in the house. Starlight looked up into the house she could not see who was in the kitchen. So she nodded to Tube to make him aware, not just that she was going now but to let him know the lights were on in the house. Tube gave himself a little shake and gave Starlight a smile.

There had been two Mouhumes looking around the garden next to Jack and Annie's. It had a lot of fruit trees and fruit bushes but was now left to wreck and ruin. What had once been a well looked after garden was now allowed to grow wild. This was not a bad thing for the Mouhumes as there was plenty of food to collect: not just the fruit that was ready now but the seeds of the fruits that had fallen to the ground, fruit that had not been eaten by the birds. The two Mouhumes looking around this garden had a lot to do. Like all creatures the Mouhumes needed variety in their diet to help keep them in good health. They did not just collect the fresh fruits but they also got the seeds still in the decaying fruits.

This was not something they liked to do but they were getting punished for something and that was their punishment. Ratty had told them to do that some seeds would be taken with Ratty for his journey. In the last two days they had been doing this punishment they had collected a lot of seeds. Some had been put to one side for Ratty and those who were going to leave with him.

Tube went on that side of the garden and stood near the hedge looking into what seemed to be a wilderness trying to spot the two Mouhumes that had been banished to do the work only in that garden. As he looked he could not see a thing. The overgrown plants could hide something as big as a large dog. It would and could definitely hide two ordinary sized Mouhumes so it was pointless trying to go in to find them.

He still stood a little longer hoping that one of them might see him but it was not to be. He would have to go to the house to see who it was and what was happening. What had been the blue light? and why had they not seen Jack in the conservatory?

Tube had told one of the Mouhumes to get some twine and attach it to a hook at the top of the window on the conservatory; he had found out about them climbing up to help the fairies. Tube knew it had all been taken down after they had made their escape, but he wanted a piece put back up and they still had not done it, so he would have to do the one thing he disliked and that was to climb the hedge. He hated climbing hedges; often if they made one mistake they would get hurt by a thorn or even get tangled and attached to parts of the hedge. That made it more difficult to try to free themselves.

As he started to climb the hedge he gave a big sigh. He began to realise that he had aged. His strength and mobility was not as it was. Not just that, but in the time they had been under the shed he had not been that active and now it was starting to show. However, he was very determined; he carried on until he reached the same level as the window. As hard as he tried to go a little higher, he ran out of steam but he was still high enough so he could see into the conservatory. The lights were on in the kitchen, he could just see someone moving around in the living room: a dark figure. He could not see who it was as there was not enough light in that room the only light that was coming in was from the kitchen and from the street light outside the front window. The curtains had not been shut.

From what he could see it looked like Annie. She was now sitting in a chair with her head buried in a coat. What was she doing Tube thought? She sat there and did not move so Tube got back down from his location. It was a lot harder going down than up. It took him some time but before he reached the bottom, where he found some Mouhumes who had been sent out to find him.

He was complaining and groaning and moaning until he saw the Mouhumes who had been sent for him. They put their arms out to help support him as he reached the bottom. It was late now so he went to the shed and told them that it would have to be in the morning when they could carry on holding their talks. However, just as he said that he could tell by their faces that they had already made their decision. He knew they had made up their minds and he could see that a large number would be leaving. A far greater number than he thought. But, he still told them he wanted to wait, to sleep on it and wait until the morning to be told what he already knew.

Chapter 22
The Decision

TUBE WAS UP early looking at the food larder. They had taken a lot out due to the rain, the Mouhumes could not go out hunting for food as much as they would have liked. The park camp had the same problem due to the bad weather. Humans had not been there so food supplies were also lower than they would have wanted.

The woodland camp had not been as bad as the other two but they also had taken out a lot from their storeroom. Tube thought this might give him a bit time to decide what he might do himself. They could not leave today as they had intended. They would have to wait until the food provisions had been topped up. He went out into in the garden. The day looked like it was going to be better than it had been.

The warm air was making vapour come from the damp earth and helping to dry it out. This was always a good indication that it was not going to rain that day. He then noticed the lights in the house had come on upstairs. Not known to Tube Annie had gone upstairs to get changed and have a wash but he knew that she would be getting ready to come down into the kitchen. That's what they done every morning then they would look out down the garden. His only concern was this ornament that Starlight and her friends had made. What would Annie think? Would she be happy or would she be annoyed? What would it also do to the harmony that had been between them until now?

Tube was right Annie was at the kitchen window looking down the garden. He hurried back to the shed and hid under it watching up the garden. He just knew that Annie would be coming down shortly. Sure enough Annie came down the garden. She looked around. What had the fairies done? Then she made a strange noise. As Mouhumes could not understand humans he did not have any idea what the noise meant. Was it good or bad? Then she did some sort of jump around the garden. What was she doing? Then off she went back up to the house.

Tube raced back to the shed to warn the others. They left quickly out of the little doorway. Some went under the shed, some went into the underground warren and others went into the little shed at the back of the garden. Just as Tube was about to go out the big door opened. Quickly he ran to find some cover but poked his head out to see who it was. In came Annie with a plate full of food, she started to speak to Tube. He could not understand what she was saying but her tone was gentle so Tube thought that he would come out to see what she wanted. After all she did have a plateful of food and she might want to give it away. It would be very handy as they did need some extra as Ratty and others were going to leave and they needed to take food.

Annie stood in one place looking around to see if she could see any Mouhumes that might be hidden away, behind something but she could not see. She was just about to go when she noticed something. Tube came out from behind a box that had lots of empty plant pots in. He gave a big stretch as he was feeling a bit stiff after he had been climbing the hedge. Then he crouched down beside the box and sat on the floor.

Annie started to talk again. Her tone was soft and kind. As she placed the plate of sandwiches on the floor in-between her and Tube. Tube gently took a sandwich and tried it. He liked it. This was not something he had tried before. It was freshly made, not something that had been put out for the birds and past its sell by date.

The side door opened; in came Ruddy but she stopped in her tracks when she saw Annie. Ruddy saw that Annie was looking at her. She had seen that Tube seemed to be fine so she started to walk backwards to the door. Tube, in a quiet voice, told Ruddy to stop and come forward. Ruddy, not saying a word, hesitated. Tube then waved his hand again as if to say come forward. At this point Annie was bending down. She must have thought that Tube had been waving to her so he held his hand out to her. To his amazement Annie copied him.

Tube picked up another sandwich and placed it onto her hand. Annie was still unsure what she should be doing or what Tube wanted her to do so she stayed still, trying to look at the two of them at the same time. Ruddy still kept her distance, as she also did not know what she should be doing. She had taken on things a lot bigger than herself but a human was more than even she could handle. All sorts of thoughts were going through her head. Would this person hurt her son Glow? Should she attack the human? Could she frighten her off if her intentions were to hurt the Mouhumes?

Tube was now pointing to Annie to give a sandwich to Ruddy and for Ruddy to take it. There was hesitation on both Ruddy and Annie's part but they did with the help of Tube. Ruddy got a hold of the sandwich and took a mouthful and straight away took another. This was something far better than they had ever had.

The Mouhume's door was slightly open and some Mouhumes were peeping through the crack. Annie stood up and started to leave the shed. Once her back was turned towards Tube and Ruddy the others came in and quickly took all the sandwiches off the plate. In no time at all they were all gone. Annie looked back she had not seen what had just happened; now all she could see was the empty plate.

A Mouhume watching from under a plant, near the top of the garden, saw her smile when she turned back towards the shed. He would report this back to Tube. It was if she was pleased to see that all the food had gone. As Annie got near the doorway of her house a man the Mouhumes had seen before but did not know who he was or his name was coming through the gate. Annie and the man stood for a while talking before they went into the house.

The Mouhume watched from his hiding place. Annie and the man went into the conservatory. The man stood at the window looking down the garden. Annie went in to the kitchen to make a drink for the two of them. She returned to the conservatory and then they sat down. As the Mouhume watched Annie and the man he could tell that what ever they were talking about was intense, just by the look on their faces. This was definitely a time when a fairy would be useful, just to help explain what the two humans were talking about. The Mouhume stayed a little longer but decided to go and tell Tube what he had seen. He also hoped to find a fairy to see if they would come back to the conservatory to see what was being said.

Back in the shed the Mouhumes shared the sandwiches amongst those who were leaving and those who were staying. They now had plenty food for the journey: maybe not as much as they would have liked but there was still sufficient and it was as much as they would be able to carry anyway. Those being left behind had enough food to last a day or two. The weather was getting better so the hunter gatherers would not be put off by the weather.

The young Mouhume who had watched Annie and the male reported back to Tube. Tube had no idea what to make of it so told everyone just to carry on as normal. Ratty and his fellow companions from the parkland and woodland camps were ready to go on their journey to find a new and satisfying land to settle in. Just like the land they once had. Could there be such a place?

They would do as they had always done: travel in small groups of about five or six. Leaving in daylight would not have been something they would have normally done but they had worked out this was the best time as humans had gone out for the day and would not be back for some time. Only a small amount of humans came back at lunchtime. They had also worked out that it would be best to leave after the morning activities had finished. It was still early so they would have to wait; besides they still did not have all their supplies sorted out. That would take a little more time as they had just been given more food.

Ruddy had been asked if she would go with Ratty. She did not sleep for days thinking about it. She was torn between Ratty and Tube. She liked them both. They were like fathers she had never known and now she was being asked to choose. No matter which one of them she chose she would be leaving the other and likely never to see him again.

The thought of it was more than she could cope with. The biggest thought going through her head was why? Why did they have to part? Why did they have to go? Why was life so hard? Why were things not straightforward? She would have to go and talk to Ratty. That was all she could do and she dreaded it, as this was a talk she hoped she would never have to have.

Ratty was under the shed amongst those who were going. They seemed well organised, had more than enough food and some had been to the pond to collect water. It ran like a military operation. All remembering that at all times they had to move in and out of the hedging keeping out of sight from all eyes.

Annie and the other human were still in the conservatory looking out of the window. They were talking but not paying much attention to what was happening outside.

Ruddy sneaked up behind Ratty and pulled him on to the ground but Ratty was quick enough to turn around on the floor and then overturn Ruddy who had not had time to pin Ratty down properly. Ruddy was laughing so much that Ratty could not tell her off. Then he started to laugh as well. The two of them had not done this for a long time. It always put Ratty in a bad mood but this time it was as if he knew this would be the last time. A tear came down his face. He wiped it off before any of the other Mouhumes had seen him. Ruddy had seen this and what she had to say would be harder than she ever thought. Ratty jumped to his feet pulling Ruddy up with him and as he did so he knew they had to talk. They went down into the shelter under the shed, as far away as they could from all the other Mouhumes.

Tube had gone outside, back to the top of the garden to watch Annie and the other human. He still needed to know what was happening. One or two of the fairies were in the hedging but Tube could not see them. Tube was still wondering what had happened to Jack? He had not been seen for a while. None of the Mouhumes had seen him either. Was this new human male now going to be a permanent fixture and if so, what impact would he have on the Mouhumes?

Tube started to think that maybe they should all go with Ratty. He also wondered, if Ratty and the others had gone and then they decided they wanted to come back that would be okay, at least they would have somewhere to come back to.

Meanwhile Ratty and Ruddy were talking. Ruddy was telling Ratty that they had everything here: plentiful supply of food, the humans Jack and Annie seemed okay and the shelter was good, as good as they could have anywhere. Then she asked, with a tear in her eye, why did he have to go? He and Tube had been on many an adventure together.

Ratty sunk his head. He had no idea why he said that he was going. He knew that if he went it would be unlikely that he would see Tube and Ruddy again. He sunk down to the ground, sitting on a rock rubbing his head.

Ruddy knew why he wanted to go as she also wanted to go for the adventure, but she knew Tube was too old for anything like that. His days had come and gone for that kind of lifestyle, especially when they had somewhere that was almost perfect.

The time had now come for all those who were leaving to congregate in and around the big shed. Tube had arrived to say his goodbyes. He was still wondering if they should all really go. With a sad heart he wished them well on their journey. So many Mouhumes had come to say goodbye.

The Mouhumes from the park and from the woodland had all come too. Tube could not believe his eyes at how many Mouhumes there were. It was truly becoming three large communities. As hard as he looked he could not see Ratty. The hustle and bustle, the coming and goings and then they were gone. An unhappy Tube walked away he needed to be alone with his thoughts.

Had he done the right thing staying? He walked around under the hedge to keep out of sight, then another hedge then another; he just walked around with his thoughts.

He had never felt like this before, yes he had lost Mouhumes who he had been friends with. But this was different. Ratty was more than a friend. How would he cope without his best friend Ratty?

He finally found a place and he sat down hoping that no one had seen him. Tears were now running down his face he was sobbing uncontrollably.

Chapter 23
The fight

THE NEXT DAY felt strange. The Mouhumes went about their day as they always did. They had been reduced in numbers and now they faced a new challenge. A Challenge where numbers would be needed something they did not have so other tactics would have to be put in place. This was something that the Mouhumes new one Mouhume would take on.

The kitten from Ted's house had caught and killed two Mouhumes earlier that morning. Some Mouhumes were still and had not known about the killing of the two Mouhumes, Tube had not been seen. He was still saddened from not seeing Ratty the day before. His friend had gone and they had not said their goodbyes. The fairies had not been seen for a while. It was as if they had been abandoned by all when they needed help most.

Ruddy was now set, she stood there dressed in her fur, her hair as golden as ever after the rain. Thorns at the ready, determination on her face, she was set to go to war with this new menace. Ruddy would not ask another Mouhume for help. This would be a fight that would or could kill her. The kitten had speed and strength, but one thing Ruddy had, was experience. Not that she had ever relied on that as each fight was always different. It was no good going into a fight with any idea other than winning.

Planning ahead as she passed another thorny bush she snapped off thorns and placed them in different locations. If she had to move around the garden she would not have time to look for more weapons. This would give her a fighting chance.

She scaled up a hedge to give her a height advantage. Then as still and as quiet as she could be she lay amongst the leaves, waiting for the kitten to come out. This was the pathway it took into Jack and Annie's garden so she had to be ready to pounce down onto it with one clean sweep.

She could hear the door being opened. Ted was telling the young cat to get out. The kitten had been getting out more now as it was getting older and Ted did not want it to be a house cat so he would let it out in the morning and let it back in lunchtime. It was learning to do what cats do and that was to hunt. Nothing more or less than the Mouhumes had done themselves.

Suddenly it was there, coming around the corner from the house it came slinking down ready to hunt. Ruddy, now with her thorns at the ready moved slowly, ready to swoop down on to the back of its neck. The kitten was moving nearer to where Rudy was. Ruddy slowly got herself into position ready to attack. She held a thorn in each hand and one in her mouth. She knew what she was going to do and what she had to do.

The young cat was getting closer now. It was also preparing to hurt or kill something, crouching down as it walked each step slowly without making a sound, it sniffed the air smelling anything that should not be there, almost into position it stopped. It stayed there not moving as if it might have known something was waiting for it. It was just out of reach for Ruddy. She still could swoop down but she would be at the disadvantage and with the kitten being bigger than her and stronger she did not want to be at any disadvantage. Her heart was not in it. She did not have that aggression that she normally had. She was thinking too much. It was not something she would do in a fight. She would generally just attack and attack and attack again until the fight was over. She gave herself a shake and told herself to stop thinking and get on with it.

The kitten changed direction and started moving again along the side of the hedge. It had not gone through the opening that it would usually go though. It was as if it was hunting something itself, Ruddy stopped for a moment to look in the direction the cat was going. She could see what it might be after. She had no time to think or hesitate. She had to move now. From branch to branch she swung jumped and leaped. There was anger on her face and aggression in her body. She jumped out of the hedge her thorns ready to do the deed

She landed just short of the back of the cat's neck onto its shoulder blades. The cat jumped up onto its back feet. Ruddy held onto its fur with one hand trying to pierce it above its shoulder but the cat was running and shaking its body trying to get her off. Then the cat did something Ruddy had not expected and that was to roll onto its back. Without hesitation, it turned one way then suddenly another. Ruddy lost her grip and landed onto the ground with a thud. It knocked the wind out of her. Suddenly the young cat was holding her down with its paw. Its claws either side of her head.

The young cat growled and with one swipe hit Ruddy's head knocking her semi unconscious. Then it picked her up with its other paw that had been holding her down and hit her again. Ruddy's body fell to the ground. The weapons she had been holding falling out of her hands. Her body lay there broken in a crumpled heap.

The cat now moved away from Ruddy it was going after the pray that it had originally intended to go after, Ruddy's son Dash. His mother had done what any mother would do without thinking and that was to defend her son. He was now hiding high up in the hedge. Dash had seen what the cat had done to his mother. Fear was something his mother had never shown, but he was feeling fear and rage as his mother was lying there not moving. From a distance you would not even think that her body was that of a Mouhume.

The cat had smashed her body so easily and now it was after Dash; Dash had learnt a lot from his mother and knew he still had a lot to learn. His hands now held a thorn, each hand holding them tight but he was fearful that he might drop one. The cat was below him sniffing the air. Dare he try and jump onto its back like his mother had tried? One thing his mother taught him was not to over think a situation, just to act without pause. Maybe that was how his mother met her end? She had not thought, but just acted. What was he to do?

Suddenly the cat pounced almost reaching him in the hedge. He almost lost his balance and had to grab hold of a branch, doing so he dropped one of his thorns. The cat quickly jumped up again hitting the branch just below him making Dash shake, almost falling out of the bush and before he could get hold of a branch to support himself It jumped again hitting another branch, only this time he fell head first lucky for Dash his clothing became snarled on the bush. This stopped him falling to his death but now he was left hanging upside down and the cat slightly out of reach was now getting more irritated.

As hard as Dash tried to get out of that position he was conscious that if he made a mistake he would fall towards the kitten and if he fell only a little more, the young cat would be able to reach him. The only thing stopping the young cat getting him were the thorns from the hedge. The cat had another idea. It started to walk back towards Ruddys body. By now there were a number of Mouhumes under the shed watching in horror. All were frozen to the spot; they all knew what the cat would do as they had seen cats do the same thing time and time again. It would go and play with the body, tossing it up and swiping it with a paw. If Ruddy was not already dead she would be soon.

The cat now stood over Ruddy's lifeless body sniffing her. Then suddenly there was a squeal from the kitten. Ruddy, with what little life was left in her with all her might had pushed a thorn under the cats chin piercing into its mouth sticking it into its tongue. The cat sped off leaving Ruddy lifeless on the ground. The Mouhumes from under the shed ran to help her. One of them had gone to tell Tube, who was now on his way. When he got into a certain position under the shed where he could see what had happened. He fell to the ground with despair.

The Mouhumes had reached Ruddy and some were helping Dash down from the hedge. Dash could only but stare in his mother's direction, hoping that she would be ok. She had cheated death so many times. He had heard all the stories about her. She must be ok but the look on those trying to help her told him something different.

Some stood crying uncontrollably. He looked around. Then he caught sight of Tube eager to see some sort of hope on his face but he was also weeping. Dash's eyes started to fill up but he was the son of Ruddy, a great worrier, brave and fearful; he could not show any weakness. His mother told him that again and again until he could stand hearing it no more.

Ruddys body was taken back under the shed. Those carrying her were still sobbing uncontrollably. Never had the Mouhumes shown such emotion openly. Ruddys body was placed down gentle with great affection.

Dash, now present along side countless Mouhumes pushed through the crowd which must have been ten deep. He stopped and took a deep breath. Even with all his strength he could not stop his eyes filling up. He bent down and held onto his mother's hand kissing it. Begging her to be ok, her body had been placed upon a brick, up off the ground it looked like an altar.

Dash still bending down felt a hand on his shoulder. He turned his head it was Ratty, Ratty had gone with the others but somewhere on the journey he knew he had to come back as Ruddy had said something to him that he could not get out of his head.

Dash stood up. Ratty put his arms around him trying to comfort him but it was also to soothe himself. He had gone into his own sleeping area and not told anyone that he was back so he was feeling guilty. He could have helped Ruddy. They might not have killed the kitten but there might not have been anymore deaths. They all stood around wondering what would happen now. There had never been anyone else like Ruddy. Not in any old tales past or present. She was something words could not explain.

Linden, Woozy, Joy and Scallop who had been spending time in the parkland warren, landed. The news had travelled fast and even those who had been some great distance away took no time in getting back. This news was even worse than their old home being destroyed. Even then Ruddy had been a leader but there was never a time when she tried to undermine Tube or Ratty. Most would have followed Ruddy, as they had done when she left the warren. Even Tube and Ratty who were the leaders, left with Ruddy. That in itself, showed her strength, not just physical but everything about her.

Dash was now standing with his head dropped down to his chest, wondering about what to do next. His fists clenched there was nothing but aggression on his face. Someone or something was going to suffer.

Bang! There was a thud on the shed wall. Buster and Tilly had arrived. Tilly using her head was banging on the site of the shed to get attention, Quickly Dash jumped up onto Tilly's back, wanting to go after the kitten. Ratty told him to get down off Tilly. That the kitten had gone home and was back in the house. Dash still wanted to go to Ted's house and barge in. maybe Tilly could open the door somehow, barking or even banging at the door. She often did that at her home. She would bark and head-butt the door. Once the door was open they could rush in and seek revenge.

Ratty told him that Tilly would be destroyed and the Mouhumes would be hunted and killed, "after all Ted took care of Ruddy when she was giving birth to you" he explained

Dash could not understand why Ted had such a creature that would kill as it did. Just as he had said that Starlight came with a number of her companions. She reached out to Dash and took him in her arms. She was a lot bigger than Dash. He seemed to disappear in her wings only his feet could be seen.

Another fairy went towards Ruddy. The Mouhumes, who had been surrounding her parted as the fairy approached Ruddy's body. She placed her hand onto Ruddy's head then spoke as she placed something over Ruddy's heart. None of the Mouhumes standing near could make out what she had said. Ruddy's hand opened ever so slightly. Those watching cheered, Dash turned around to see what the excitement was. His mother was breathing. Her chest was moving ever so slightly but moving. She had taken a beating, a beating that would have killed most creatures and one that almost killed her.

Ruddy would need to rest, she would need to build her strength up, Starlight told them that when Ruddy was ready they would have to go and see the young cat and try and make peace, just as she had done with all the other creatures in that area.

Glow arrived. She had been away with her son Capheus. It was that time, when they would part and would never see each other again. That had been the reason the Mouhumes had not seen the fairies. It had been a sad few days for them. A new male had arrived and he would be welcomed later that day, but first Starlight and Glow had to persuade Tube and Ratty that they had the best interest for Ruddy and they must do as they were asked and do only what they would be told to do. They knew they must do what ever it took and that they would have to start straight away to help Ruddy to survive, Tube, without hesitation agreed; Ratty was unsure but went along with what was being said. They would have to move her with care to somewhere that they could attend to her. Glow and Starlight could not go into the Mouhumes underground camp.

Mousy came and Starlight took him to one side. She told him that he must keep everyone away except those who would be picked to help with her needs. She then pointed to the fairy that had touched Ruddy. Starlight did not give her name or even say who she was, but it was clear that she was someone important and that she held a higher status than all those who they had already met.

They decided where she would be placed and who would watch over her, Tube and Ratty were chosen to watch over her. They were told that no other Mouhume would or could enter the area that had been chosen for her. No matter what or how long it took.

Chapter 24
The Following Week

OVER THE NEXT few weeks Ruddy was in recovery. None of the Mouhumes had any idea on how to help a sick Mouhume. It would be a case of letting nature taking its course and only the strongest would survive.

This time they had help, the fairy community had knowledge of sickness and ill health. They had what the Mouhumes thought, magical powers; after all they could make themselves vanish. So what other mysterious things could they do, bring back the dead as it seemed they had done with Ruddy!

Tube and Ratty had stayed near Ruddy watching over her in the small shed at the back of the garden. They had taken Ruddy there because the fairies could not go under the ground. The openings were too small for them and they could damage their wings. The fairy that had stroked Ruddy over her head when she was all but dead came every day to tend to her. But when she came in to the room Tube and Ratty had to leave. This was the only time they left her side.

They had been given strict orders of what they must do and not do. They followed the instructions to the letter. After all, this was Ruddy. No other Mouhume had been given permission to go anywhere near her, not even Dash could see his mother. Dash had asked Tube and Ratty why, but they could not answer, not even they knew why the fairies had said that no one could see her. All they could say was she was getting better each day and with every new day she was getting stronger.

Ruddy was getting visits not just from this new fairy but her old friends Starlight and Glow. They came with foods and other things. Things Tube and Ratty could not know about. They were not allowed to see what they had or what they were doing.

Though each time Tube and Ratty were allowed back in to see her they could see a difference, in a good way and each time she was getting stronger. Today was the first time they had seen her sit up. She was still looking weak but compared to just a few days earlier there was a big difference and all for the better. She was still not talking. Tube and Ratty had been told not to try and talk to her so they did precisely as they had been asked. Unknown to them Ruddy had also been told not to talk but just point to what she wanted or needed.

All would become clear in a day or two. Glow had told them that the fairy looking after Ruddy would explain all they wanted to know. As Glow told them this she had a sadness about her. It was as if she knew it was not going to be good news.

Glow went on to tell them that Dash would be allowed to see his mother the next day and they must tell him that he could talk but not to encourage Ruddy to talk. They were also told that the fairy who was helping Ruddy to recover would be there to make sure her demands would be carried out. Glow said this with manner and tone in her voice. Glow also advised them that if this was not carried out exactly as they had been told then things would not be okay. Ratty wanted to ask why, but it was as if he knew he would not be told, so all he could do was nod his head to show he understood.

Starlight and the fairy that were looking after Ruddy were in the shed. Tube had arrived back, he had been away checking up on the other Mouhumes, making sure they were still doing what they needed to do and also asking about the kitten. No one had seen the kitten since that day.

Tube also asked about Jack, whether anyone had seen him? They told Tube none of them had seen Jack, they had seen Annie coming and going out of the house but that she had not been down the garden. The other human had been once or twice but not in the house so they just hid. The human had looked around the sheds and the garden but that was all he had done. He was just looking, he never touched anything.

Tube did not know what to make of this. Who was he and what had happened to Jack? Annie was always coming and going out of the house so that was nothing knew but who was this human?

Starlight was just coming out of the shed when Tube arrived. He asked what had happened to the young cat. Starlight told him after Ruddy stabbed it under the chin it had not been out of the house. Its chin had swollen up so it was being kept in the house until the wound had healed.

Tube reported this news to all the other Mouhumes. Once again, Ruddy had saved their lives. Once again, she had put all other lives before her own. This time it had been far more than any … number of Mouhumes could have … he stopped, he could not carry on. All those there knew what he wanted to say. No matter how many Mouhumes would have or could have stood up to the cat they could not have done any better and most would have been more than likely killed.

Tube had also asked the name of the fairy taking care of Ruddy. Starlight could only tell him that the name she had been given many years ago. It was not something she wanted to share. Only a small number knew her name but what she could tell him was that she had spent some time with humans and learned a lot of things just by watching and listening. She was now full of knowledge.

One thing she had said was not to be too quick in trusting humans. This had Tube thinking, why then did they trust Ted so much? What was the name of this fairy he had never seen until now? Why did she not trust humans? So many thoughts and questions were going through his head but one thing was sure, she was helping to making Ruddy better.

Each day she would bring food. Some of which he recognised and some he had never seen before. There were ointments that he had no idea about. This was something the Mouhumes did not do, treat an injured Mouhume. They would have to get better by themselves. It wasn't that they did not want to help injured Mouhumes but they had no idea how to do it or what they had to do.

A wounded Mouhume often died from wounds, if not from the wound itself, the infection would often finish them off. As for broken bones, again infection or out of place bones would be the end of them.

Ruddy was needed. They would have tried anything to keep her safe. Even though they would not have known what they were supposed to do. This fairy seemed to know what to do. She had it all in order. She cleaned Ruddy flesh wounds. She knew exactly what rest was needed, any slight exercise and when she had done too much. Tube and Ratty might not have been there when she was doing what she did but they still had some idea what was happening. They should have asked what the food stuff was and how it would help her but they said nothing.

A week passed and Ruddy was now standing by herself although she was still a little unsteady on her feet. Each day she was looking better. Ruddy had wanted to go out amongst the other Mouhumes but she was advised not to, for another day at least.

The fairy explained to her that she needed to look as strong as she had done before the fight. This would give the Mouhumes hope. Then it suddenly became clear to Ruddy. After all she had seen and done this many times before. She had seen all the signs and now she knew what had been happening. This was not going to be a long-term fix but only for show: a show that could only be for a short time. How long she had no idea about.

Starlight came in the shed with Glow. Ruddy asked them why had they saved her? Why not let her die. Why all of this just to prolong things? They sank their heads. This was not going to be easy for them. But they could only tell her the truth as they seen it.

It had started some days earlier when they were at the pond and the young cat came. All the fairies could do was to go for the dogs to help the Mouhumes. Though it had only been Buster they could get at that time and it was only then they knew that something would have to be done so that they all could live in harmony.

Starlight and Glow and even others had tried to talk to the young cat. But like all cats it was built in to them to hunt. The kitten had killed at least three fairies and two Mouhumes in the last few days when it had been allowed out of the house.

It might live in Ted's house but it belonged to Ted's wife Linda. They told Ruddy that Linda had no idea about the fairies never mind all the Mouhumes. It had not been something Ted had ever told her.

"So when Linda got the young cat Ted did not think that it would hurt any of us, not even thinking about the Mouhumes but then he had just seen you Ruddy and then you had your boy Dash," Ruddy nodded.

"Ted had helped in a way. He brought food out and let the fairies look after you, so he had not been a bad human. Jack on the other hand, had left traps that killed one of the Mouhumes then put lights in the garden that could have put the Mouhumes at risk"

The three fairies stayed with Ruddy to explain about her wounds and broken bones. What was likely to happen and that she would never be the same as she had been. Then they told Ruddy what they would like her to do and what she might be able to do once they had her on her feet … but that would be at least another day or two.

Chapter 25
Alliance

IT HAD BEEN nearly two weeks since the parting of the Mouhumes and Ruddy's recovery. Still no one had seen her. The young cat had only been out once since the fight. Since that day nothing had come into the garden that would hurt the Mouhumes.

Some Mouhumes had now worked out a routine to go between the other camps. That way they could help each other and learn about different things. The woodland Mouhumes had different creatures living alongside them, some they would rather not have had anywhere near them, while others had been a good food supply. The same went for the parkland Mouhumes. The food source was similar as the garden Mouhumes. Most of the food came from humans but they also had fish and a few different animals that they could eat and also be eaten by.

So it was good that the three camps kept in contact with each other as they were able to learn about what was happening, what was the best way to do some things and what dangers were about. Although most of all, they were able to make sure all camps had support when it was needed. They all wanted to know about Ruddy: how she was and whether she had been seen outside yet? That was always the first question anyone asked when any of the Mouhumes from the garden camp dropped by even if they were just visiting. Sometimes when the Mouhumes went between the camps they would often stay overnight, sometimes two nights. It was something they had just started to do. That way they could learn more about one another's environments.

They also brought each other food which meant because they had different types of food; it would give them all a better diet. Not always a healthier diet but a different one. Those in the park often had leftover food from the takeaway shop: like chips, kebab and pieces of different flavoured pies but most of the time they left chips.

Parts of the parkland had berries growing but not enough to sustain the growing numbers. The food the humans threw away was more than enough to store away for bad weather. They had learned in a short time that when the weather was not good the humans did not come to the park so they had to store as much as they could rotating it to help keep it edible.

Word had got around that Ruddy was back on her feet and on top of the agenda a meeting with the young cat to be made although it was unclear if Ruddy was going to kill the young cat; especially since she had nearly done so at the last meeting. This time she would have help, no Mouhume wanted any harm to come to her again.

The strongest from the park and the strongest from the woodland went to the garden where Ruddy was but when they got there they had been told the meeting was with Ruddy and Ruddy alone. This was not something any of the Mouhumes had wanted but they were told it was for the welfare of the community.

It was true enough, after they arrived and the meeting was about to start, Ruddy was back on her feet looking as strong as ever. She was covered in fur from top to bottom but unknown to any other Mouhume that was to hide the wounds and battle scars.

Ruddy went with Glow, Starlight and another fairy, not the one who had helped her back to health but another one, who looked far stronger than any other fairy they had seen before. She made Ruddy look weak next to her.

Dash stood watching his mother being led away. He had been told by Tube and Ratty not to intervene in any way. This instruction had come from his mother. Tube and Ratty, one on each side of Dash, did not know the full reason for this meeting. All had been kept secret. Only Ruddy and the fairies knew what was going to happen.

Ruddy had her thorns tucked under her fur tied around her waist. She had more covering than normal but still looked good. She walked with a slight limp but hid it well under her clothes.

As she entered the meeting area, arranged by the new fairy with the strict face, Ruddy looked around towards Starlight. Starlight was looking nervous as did Glow. This made Ruddy a bit apprehensive. She placed a hand on one of her thorns ready to pull out and attack.

The place chosen was only two gardens away. It had an area that was overgrown but also had an area with short cut grass. This was ideal for the meeting and the overgrown area would be a good escape if need be.

The kitten came. It was crouching down, as cats do when they are ready to attack. Ruddy was just about to pull out her thorn when her hand was stopped. Starlight placed her hand on top of Ruddy's. Ruddy's first instinct was to pull out the other one with her other hand but Glow was on that side and placed her hand on top of the handle. What were they doing? Why had they stopped her?

The kitten was now encircling Ruddy. Its jaw area still had some swelling around it where Ruddy had stabbed it. Its claws were already out and its teeth were showing. It was a frightening sight, not just for Ruddy but Starlight and Glow too, who had now made themselves invisible.

The only fairy that could be seen was the one who had come with them. As big as she was the young cat still looked more powerful. The fairy jumped in front of the kitten startling it. It stopped in its tracks, moving slightly back. Ruddy had seen this happen before. When cats do this they sometimes pounce forward.

The fairy put her hand on the kitten's nose with her palm over its nostrils and pushed hard downwards. The kitten seemed to just lie down and wagged its tail with temper, not really knowing what was happening but unable to do anything. Then Ruddy was beckoned over to the kitten's head. Starlight and Glow showed themselves again but stood back, away from Ruddy.

Ruddy stood over the helpless kitten. The fairy pointing to her as if to kill it; Ruddy was a little confused. She pulled her thorn out and looked at the kitten that was now unable to move. What had the fairy done to stop this killing machine in its tracks? It had killed one, if not more fairies, so how was it, all of a sudden, helpless just by one touch?

The fairy asked Ruddy why she had not killed it. Ruddy could not kill something that she or any other Mouhume was not in danger from. The kitten's claws had been out ready to attack but now they were not to be seen. It had pulled its claws back. It could only look with its eyes and unable to move its head.

Ruddy shook her head. She could not kill it. The fairy asked again.

"Why? It would have killed you"

Then she told Ruddy that she would be dead now if not for the care she had so why not kill the enemy that had killed your kind. She asked again with a little more harshness in her voice.

Ruddy told her she did not kill for any other reason other than for food or to survive. She did not kill for killing sake. The fairy then asked what she would like her to do with the kitten. Ruddy, as always, told her the kitten could be good friends like your kind have been, like the two dogs Buster and Tilly have been and the hedgehog. She wanted them all to get along.

The fairy then reminded Ruddy that cats have killing built in them. They can't help themselves; it's something they just do. Not necessarily for badness or even to eat, it's just something they must do.

Ruddy stood for a while thinking about everything she had been told. She knew it was true but all of her new friends once, if not all, had a fight with her and almost killed her, apart from the two dogs.

She looked at the fairy and asked if she could tell the kitten she did not want to harm it and at the same time she did not want her friends harmed. She also wanted to know if it was possible for them all to get along. She said there was plenty to hunt and kill.

The fairy told Ruddy she did not need to tell the kitten anything as the kitten could understand everything that was said. She also told Ruddy that when she had put her hand on the kitten she had something in her hand that would make the cat understand what was happening and what was being said, but at the same time helpless.

"So how will we know if it will be a friend or enemy? And how will we deal with it?" Ruddy asked.

The fairy told Ruddy there is only one way we can do this to find out and that was to remove what ever hold she has on the kitten. As she said this she tapped the kitten on its head. The kitten pounced up and gave Ruddy a fright but Ruddy, unlike normal, did not pull out her thorn ready to fight. She just stood there.

The young cat, after hearing all that had been said, now had a choice to make. It walked from side to side, looking all the time at Ruddy. Both did not say a word. Ruddy did not move her head, only her eyes kept watch.

Then the young cat jumped onto Ruddy, knocking her down with its paws and pinned her arms. All the aches and pains she thought had gone came back twice as hard. Even if she wanted to fight she could not. It looked straight into her eyes and was only a breath away from her face. The young cat said that it liked to play and it liked to hunt.

This was strange; Ruddy could understand what it was saying. Ruddy still pinned down looked towards the fairy with surprise on her face. Obviously the fairy knew why Ruddy was looking surprised. How was it she could understand the kitten now?

Ruddy, without showing any fear, told the kitten the Mouhumes also like to play and liked to fight but they did not have to kill everything they came into contacted with. The kitten let her up and then started to walk away. As it did so it said they could get along and there would be no more killing of Mouhumes or fairies.

Chapter 26
Annie

ANNIE HAD STARTED to come down the garden again. She had been missing for a while. The Mouhumes had not seen a lot of her until now. It had always been Jack who ventured into the garden but lately it had just been Annie. Until recently she had just been seen as someone who went into the house then out the next day. She was always just seen very briefly but now she was the only one who was seen regularly.

Sometimes she was seen with another man sitting in the conservatory, both of them looking out to the garden as they chatted. That was all the man did, look out. Once he had tried to come around the pond but the Mouhumes hid away. They did not want another human near them at this time. So the man kept his distance, it was as if he knew that was what they wanted.

Annie did not just bring food for them. She also started to make clothes for them from materials she had around the house. Some things she knitted and others she stitched from old clothes. The Mouhumes still had to modify some garments but most were just right.

The fairies still kept out of sight from Ted's wife, Linda. They were still unsure about Annie so they tried to keep out of her sight. Every now and again they forgot about her and went about their jobs as normal. They watched Annie but they mostly stayed hidden away to see what was happening and what was being said when Annie was in the conservatory with the man.

They still had little idea of who he was and why, when he came, all he did was to sit and watch the Mouhumes. Sometimes he had something on a stand that he had pointing towards the pond and sometimes down the garden towards the shed and greenhouse. The Mouhumes had no idea what it might be but it didn't seem to hurt anything in the garden so they weren't that concerned.

The man was coming at different times of the day and more and more with his stand. They tried to find out what it might be but when Annie and the man talked it was mainly about Jack. What they had discovered was that Jack was in something called a hospital. They had heard the man asking Annie when Jack would be out of hospital.

They had not heard what Annie had said. So they had no idea what a hospital was or when Jack was coming back. It seemed to be a long time since Jack had been seen so hearing his name was a good thing. The fairy, Lilac, was the one who kept an eye on Annie. She informed the Mouhumes what was being said and also told Starlight and Glow.

The fairies learned about the human who had been coming to the house. He was called Brian and he was a friend of Jack and Annie. Lilac watched over Annie almost all day and best part of the night. She understood most of the things said by humans but she still did not know everything such as hospital and a few other words.

Lilac was keen on learning as much as she could about human beings. It was good for her to study Annie. Lilac overheard Jack was coming home in two days. Annie had been telling Brian that he was being brought home the night before the funeral and that Jack was going to go into the living room.

Brian had been asking Annie what had happened. Annie told Brian that Jack had been suffering for a long time and being caught in the rain knocked him back. Then he went into some sort of depression and with everything else he caught pneumonia too.

Lilac had no idea what Annie had said but she could remember most of what had been discussed. She also noticed Annie looked very emotional when she was talking about this to Brian. Then suddenly she smiled and cheered her self up asking Brian to help her to move some furniture in the living room.

As the two of them moved the furniture around Annie was talking all the time about Jack and how he would be put in a certain position so that he could look out towards the conservatory. She had Brian moving things around then putting them back. Then she had Brian take a small table upstairs and a little while later it was brought back down again. They stopped for a drink. It was if Annie had finally realized Brian was worn out. He was not a young man nor was he a fit man, all this hard work showed on his face. So when she asked him if he wanted a drink he was only to glad to accept.

Brian walked back into the conservatory. He stood for a while looking down the garden towards the shed. Then he looked at the little box on top of the tall stand, took it off placed it on his knee and sat down looking at it.

Lilac could not understand what he was doing but his face seemed to light up when he was looking at it. Annie came in with drinks for them. Annie asked about the little box. Brian showed it to Annie. They both smiled. What ever it was seemed to bring them happiness. Brian put it back. This time pointing it slightly towards the fish pond. Lilac shrugged her shoulders and dismissed it. Humans were strange!

Annie started to talk about Jack again and started to cry. "The things that Jack could do before his accident he can no longer do and the harder he tried the more upset he got."

Lilac had never seen a human cry before. She then knew that something bad must had happened to Jack. Lilac herself felt upset seeing Annie cry whilst trying to tell Brian.

Starlight came to the side of Lilac. Lilac started to tell Starlight what had happened, what she could understand and even what she had little idea about. She knew she had to repeat the words that Annie had said to Brian. Lilac started from the beginning. Annie had told Brian that Jack had been in a car crash a number of years ago. He had got himself back to work but irritated a part of his injury that had happened in the crash. Lilac had little idea what some of these words meant but she continued repeating it word for word. She had a good memory.

Jack needed an operation to repair the damage and then he needed another operation on his heart. Even before that he had been in a lot of pain. When moving around he would get bad-tempered or even aggressive. The more pain he was in the less he would tell anyone and the more he would try to get back to normal the less he could. It was a vicious circle. Then he would get irritable, driving friends and family away. The last few days she had spent with Jack had been the longest and that was only because they had been watching the Mouhumes … Lilac then stopped. She got a lump in her throat. This was not something the fairies had ever experienced. Could this be an emotion they had never had?

As Lilac was telling Starlight it became clear that things right in front of humans can be missed. Things they should have seen but just overlooked, much like the fairies. This puzzled Lilac. How could humans not see something right in front of them?

Brian was still in the house with Annie. He had gone into the kitchen area to make a fresh drink for Annie who had now stopped crying. To the side of Annie was a little table with some outfits on she had made for the Mouhumes. She made tops and bottoms. They were all different. She had clearly kept herself busy.

She must have made ten or more outfits for the Mouhumes. All were put in a neat pile of tops and bottoms. Then just behind that pile was another pile but different styles and colours. She must have used anything she had to make clothes with.

She had not put them out for the Mouhumes yet. She had been distracted with Jack. It had been sudden. It looked like he was going to make a recovery but then he took a turn for the worst. It took Annie by surprise. As he seemed to be on the mend she had not gone to hospital that day to see him. She had things to do at home and now she was feeling guilty.

Chapter 27
The Funeral and Starlight

STARLIGHT STARTED TO keep an eye on Annie. Starlight stayed with her for days on end, watching over her. She had never seen a human in mourning but it was not that different to the time when Glow parted with her son, Capheus. She could actually understand the hurt and pain she was going through.

Not all Annie said was understood. Some words were new to the fairy. There were people coming and going. Starlight had never seen as many humans going to Jack and Annie's home. They were all saying similar things and Annie continued to tell them the same account. Sometimes it was slightly different but always about Jack and how he had passed away.

Starlight had never had a lot to do with Jack and Annie. She had seen Jack before his accident in the garden. He cared for the plants and his fish. He looked like he had a kindness about him and she noticed how he liked things in order: such as his garden tools. He put them away after he had used them. He cleaned them, oiled them and did what ever else he needed to do.

The human Brian had not been for a number of days. Lots of other humans were bringing flowers and cards. Starlight could not read what was on the cards but they gave her something to hide behind, the flowers did too.

The day had come to say goodbye to Jack. His body was in a coffin in the living room. Humans came to speak to Jack in private whilst others stood in the kitchen and others stayed in the dining room or the conservatory. Even some of the humans stood outside in the garden. Starlight told the Mouhumes what was happening and what she thought it meant. The Mouhumes hid amongst the flowers.

Starlight had been upstairs in the bedroom where Annie was getting herself ready. Annie was sitting on the edge of the bed sobbing. Starlight felt the pain that Annie must have been feeling as she, just a few days earlier, had to say goodbye to Capheus.

Jack was in his coffin, they had left it open only showing Jack from his waist up to his head. Some of the Mouhumes had sneaked in to see

Jack and it all became clear. This was the first time the Mouhumes and the fairies had seen a dead human. A new understanding had come to them: humans also die and they too find it hard when it happens.

Cars pulled up outside and there were men in black clothing. They walked in and spoke to Annie. Annie nodded and they went into the room where Jack was. Those in and around the other rooms went outside. They lined up along the garden footpath and some lined up the path outside the garden.

The men, who had gone into the room where Jack had been, now came out carrying the coffin, then they placed it into one of the cars. Annie came out behind them and climbed into another car; just behind the one Jack had been placed in. followed by some other humans, Ted and Linda also climbed in. The street was full of humans; they were all in dark clothing. As the cars drove off slowly one of the humans walked in front of the cars. The fairies placed themselves in the street.

The Mouhumes were also there hiding in and amongst the plants, up and down the street. This had been the first time the Mouhumes were out in numbers hidden amongst humans.

The cars took a little time to drive away. They were almost out of sight before the man walking in front got into the car. It then drove away at a slightly faster pace. The rest of the humans who had stood outside the house got into their cars and drove away.

Starlight was still in the bedroom looking out the window, a tear rolled down her cheek. It was a sadness she knew only too well. As the last car went out of sight she went downstairs. Some of the windows were still open. The conservatory door was slightly open. Someone must have pushed it closed but not sufficiently enough for it to catch shut.

This gave Starlight an idea. How could she help Annie? What could she and the Mouhumes do to take some of this pain away for Annie? She called out for some of the Mouhumes to come into the house. They all went into the dining room which adjoined the kitchen.

Starlight asked the Mouhumes to look around the house for anything that seemed out of place. She explained what she meant. She took them into the room where Jack had been and pointed to the floor. It had bits of broken plants on the carpet.

That would be the first room they would tidy up. They picked up the broken stems from the flowers and anything else that might have been dropped on to the floor. They also picked up bits of paper and flower petals. Before they got started you could hardly see the carpet for all the bits on the floor.

They cleared it in no time, putting all the rubbish in the bin outside. As for the cups and other things in the kitchen the Mouhumes put them in the sink. Turning the tap was more than a task. They had no idea how to do it so they left it alone. At least the kitchen tops were tidy!

They did as much as they could to help Annie. Some things were just too heavy for the fairies and the Mouhumes to move so they just had to leave them as they were. Annie would most likely not notice due to her being so upset. It would give her something to do when she got back home.

That was all they could do for now. Just before they were leaving they went around the house to check that everything was alright: that all windows were locked and doors were shut. Then they went out of the conservatory door. That was the only door not locked. Starlight could see the door had a key in it. She asked the Mouhumes to push it shut from the outside as the door, when opened, it went outwards not inwards.

Starlight could not work out who had closed that door and why they had only pushed it so that it looked shut. Something worried Starlight. There had been people there she had not seen before. Starlight had been around Ted's for a number of years. She knew all the faces around that street and those who passed through but there had been some faces she had never seen. She asked for Tube to come with Ratty and Ruddy. She needed to see them urgently.

The Mouhume went for Tube, Ratty and Ruddy without hesitation. Starlight needed to know something. She had a suspicion about something she had seen before but she just wanted to make sure that it was not her imagination.

She stayed in the house until Tube and Ratty landed. Ruddy was not that far behind them. To Ruddy's surprise Starlight looked worried. They started to talk about the day's events. She asked if any of them had seen who was last to come out of the conservatory door? Tube had seen. He explained who it was. It was someone who often went in houses and garden sheds. The Mouhumes had seen him a number of times.

Starlight wanted to know more about this human. Tube started to tell her that he was well known to the Mouhumes. He was often seen going into houses that were empty. What he meant to say was that when a home owner had gone out he would often go inside. Sometimes coming out with items and putting them into a car waiting nearby.

Starlight then knew the Mouhumes did not know about this type of human. She started to tell them of the type of human he was and that she thought Annie might be in danger. She asked Tube and Ratty to get as many Mouhumes willing to help defend Annie's home. Ruddy just looked at Starlight. Starlight put her hand up and asked Ruddy if she would be the eyes and ears on the ground. Ruddy nodded. Starlight knew that Ruddy was still not at full strength. She was not sure if she would ever be again.

Countless fairies came. They hid themselves all around the house and outside, near the doorway. The Mouhumes came thorns in each hand. Starlight looked at them. They needed something else. Thorns in their hands would not be enough. Then it came to her. She had been around at Ted's one day: he had been watching the television and she had seen something that might be useful.

She told a number of fairies what she wanted. Quickly they flew off. The light outside was dulling and the sky was filling up with clouds. She needed to tell the Mouhumes what she was wanted them to do. She was determined to protect Annie's home.

Tube and Ratty were standing nearby. Starlight was talking quietly. Ruddy could hardly make out what was being said. Then the fairies came back. They had not been away long. They had things in their hands: some had long sticks and others had shorter sticks. How was this going to help thought Ruddy.

Starlight told Tube and Ratty she would show them what to do but she needed everything back when it was over. Tube and Ratty agreed but could not understand what all the fuss was about, they often used long sticks!

The fairies then started to bend the longer sticks. They attached some cord, turning it around so it was pointing towards the cushion on the chair. With a shorter stick they placed it onto the cord then pulled it back as far as they could then let go. The Mouhumes jaws must have dropped with amazement.

They had never seen anything like it before. They never even thought that two sticks of different lengths could be so effective. The cushion was covered in sticks sticking out. Tube was the first to go and look at the cushion. Some sticks had almost gone all the way through. Just the end of the stick was sticking out of the cushion. Ruddy stood with her mouth wide open. She was amazed by what she had just seen.

Starlight told them that she only had seven of these new killing weapons and she wanted them back afterwards. They all agreed. The Mouhumes that were going to use these weapons came forward. Starlight explained what she wanted them to do.

She showed them what to do. She held the longer stick with the string attached to it in the middle then she placed the smaller stick in her hand, attaching it to the string. She then told them to pull the stick as far back as they could. With her arm slightly bent she then told them to look down the stick to the end of the tip. Then once they saw what they wanted to hit they had to let it go.

TWANG! They hit the target with a thud. Starlight pointed to the pillow. Now it was the Mouhumes turn. Six had bows. She explained the larger sticks are called bows and the shorter stick is called an arrow.

They took their turns: some were dropping the bows after they had let go of the arrow. The string had scraped up their forearms. This was not something they had expected. Now they were rubbing their arms and jumping around the room in pain. Starlight started to laugh. She had forgotten to tell them about the string sometimes catching the forearms.

Those who had dropped the bows did not want to have another go so others had to try. Ruddy was one of them. She had seen what had happened to those who had not held the bow correctly. She picked the bow up and held it like Starlight showed them, bending her arm slightly holding the bow. She placed the string onto the arrow groove then pulled back as far as she could. She had not expected it to be as hard to pull back the cord. It took some strength.

She looked down the arrow as she had been told then let go of the cord. Thud, it hit the target right where Ruddy had aimed for. She was thrilled with her aim. Starlight came to her side and was beaming at Ruddy's achievement.

Six of the Mouhumes who wanted to try these new weapons had now been picked. Starlight was holding one too. She told them if they needed to fire them, to do altogether. Tube asked what they were going to be shooting.

Starlight told them the man that had left the doorway unlocked because he was a thief. She had seen him go in and out of human homes many times, taking things that did not belong to him and she thought that he was intending to come back to take Annie's possessions. The next question was as important as anything could possibly be.
 "Do we kill him?" asked Ruddy.

"No we just shoot him in his legs and backside area, that should put him off," Starlight said. She had no sooner said those words when one of the Mouhumes came running in telling them that a human was coming towards the house. He had come from the woodland area and through one of the gardens on the other side of the road.

They all hid away. The gate slightly squeaked as it opened. The conservatory door was pulled open. A dark figure snuck into the conservatory. The Mouhumes and fairies were all hidden away but peeping out to see what was happening. The human went into the living room towards the television quickly bending down to unplug it. As he did so the Mouhumes shot their arrows simultaneously into his backside.

He squealed a squeal that would have been heard streets away. The human's body straightened up as he screamed. Starlight with her bow and arrow was just behind him: twang ... her arrow was let go. It went right into the middle of his ear, straight through. There was another yell and he was off running out the way he had come in. Not known to him, the fairies and the Mouhumes set another trap. They had string attached on to the gate posts, just high enough to make him trip on to all sorts of prickly things.

The human fell face down onto the palms of his hands and some sharp objects. Not just that, some Mouhumes could not resist in stabbing him in the legs with thorns. The human was up on to his feet, almost running before his feet were off the ground. It was a frightening experience for him, one that he would never forget.

The fairies and the Mouhumes started to tidy up the footpath and in the house where they had left evidence that they had been there. It was getting late and they knew Annie would be coming back some time soon.

They wanted everything just right for her but they also did not want her to know what had gone on. This was something the Mouhumes could not understand: how one creature could do something so wrong to another creature. Starlight started to tell them as they were tiding up. She had seen a number of things that humans did to one another that would not be done by any other living thing.

Car lights pulled up outside and then the car door opened. The Mouhumes could see that Annie had returned. Annie was getting out the car, as she did so she was talking to the driver. She then stood outside the car stretching and straightening her back but then bending slightly to talk to the driver once again.

The Mouhumes could not understand what was being said but it all seemed pleasant enough. Not moving they stayed hidden away, forgetting to go and tell those in the house. Annie was heading towards the back door when one of the Mouhumes realized that those in the house should have been told. It was not that Annie had not seen them before; it was just so they knew she was coming.

Annie walked in, almost straight into Starlight who was telling the Mouhumes to put the bows and arrows away. Starlight was hovering almost at the same height as Annie. Annie stopped in mid tracks not taking her eyes off Starlight. Starlight still hovering; looked into Annie's eyes forgetting she could no longer use her energy to make herself invisible. She could do nothing about it. It was something she had never wanted, to be seen by another human. All the time she had been with Ted, Ted's wife, Linda had never seen any of the fairies.

Annie smiled and stuck out her hand, with one of her fingers pointing outwards indicating to Starlight if she wanted to rest on it she could. Starlight had seen Annie many times before. She knew she was not a bad person and her energy was low now so she rested on Annie's finger. She looked straight into Annie's eyes, Annie might have been smiling slightly but her eyes could not hide the pain that she was feeling. Annie's eyes were full of tears. Starlight's eyes also filled up, it was if she could sense Annie's pain. It looked like it was going to be the beginning of a new friendship.

The End

If you liked this story you also might like

**Jack and Annie's
Magical garden**

Watch out for

Annie's Magical new friends

Homeless (*play*)

Order in the court (*play*)

Printed in Poland
by Amazon Fulfillment
Poland Sp. z o.o., Wrocław